The Third Dawn

From Bethlehem to Golgotha

Thomas J. Nichols

Nicholson Books

ISBN-13: 979-8-9883672-1-5 (Paperback)

ISBN-13: 979-8-9883672-0-8 (eBook)

ISBN-13: 979-8-9883672-5-3 (Hardback)

Cover design by KJ Waters Consultancy (KJWConsultancy.com) and Jody Smyers Photography (JodySmyersPhotography.com).

Also By Thomas J. Nichols

Color of the Prism
We Were Young Once...
The Russian
Voices in the Fog
The Spy Among Us
Arrows of Allah
Sweet Emily
Other works are published short stories
Noble Generation II
Short Stories by Texas Authors

Contents

Preface

Writing a novel on the life of Jesus Christ has not been easy. The back-story to where we are today with a bible-based fiction for readers of all ages is a story in itself.

I suffered from severe asthma as a child. With minimal outdoor play activity and being too young and unable to read, I "looked at" what we called "the funny papers" of The Kansas City Star. The dialogue was not a problem. I was creative and made up the words, whether spoken by Li'l Abner, Dick Tracy, or Sky King. In my mind, I was "reading" the funnies. The silver lining to that dark era of my life was the development of long-term skills in creative writing.

St. Joseph's Boys School, Tucson, Arizona

When I was near death, Catholic nuns offered my parents the one alternative that might save my life: Move to the desert and away from the humidity and pollen of Kansas City, Missouri. In a last-ditch effort, my mother took me to St. Joseph's Boys School, an orphanage on aptly named Orphanage Road, in Tucson, Arizona. It worked.

Creative writing was in my blood from those previous years, and with guidance from my wife, I graduated magna cum laude from the University of Arizona. As my career grew, I graduated from the FBI National Academy, FBI Leadership Program, the Senior Management Institute for Police at Harvard, and many other programs and universities.

Strong family relationships, equally strong bonds with our Christian faith, and our continued pledge to civic activity have kept our family close to each other, our community, and our religious faith.

Upon retirement, I turned to what has been an integral part of my life—I write. With five decades of criminal justice history, I have many stories to tell. I add to that vast memory bank with the role religion played in my life.

That brings us to now—my creative venture into the personal life of Jesus, the Nazarene.

Introduction

The Roman Empire of approximately five million square kilometers encompassed the world from Britannia to Mauretania, Egypt and Syria, Mesopotamia, northward to Armenia and across the Danube to Dacia. The Roman authorities maintained a military force of soldiers, cavalry, Praetorian Guard, and allies of approximately 500,000 men, plus their facilities, horses, and hardware to preserve order. The expenditures for their military might, and the lifestyles of the pompous and arrogant were a significant drain on their treasury. Roman taxation was broadscale to maintain a positive cash flow. Publicans (tax collectors) collected taxes on every head, animal, vine, land, or any other asset. There were no exemptions—Jew, Gentile, Roman, barbarian, male or female, freeman or slave. A person's death did not necessarily exempt them from the publican. In some locales, depending on a region's wealth or poverty, the deceased's family had to pay that person's tax.

This was the geo-political atmosphere in the era of Jesus, the Nazarene.

Chapter One
The Orphan

The shadows of Mount Tabor crept across the desert floor toward the city. A young boy clad in a calf-length grey tunic, belt, and sandals glanced over his shoulder as he entered the synagogue grounds. From this moment forward, he will be at the heart and soul of events that will transform the future of the human race.

Nearby in their home, Anne and Joachim, the soon-to-be grandparents of Mary's baby, settled in for their evening meal. Unbeknownst to them, a youngster had trekked across the deserts of Samaria and Galilee to deliver a message from the Eternal Father to them.

Joachim lowered himself onto the cushion alongside the table and bade his wife to join him. The house servants, Rachel and Nadab, served wine in elegant clay cups, dried fish, goat cheese, and a fresh pomegranate and melon to each of them, then retired to their quarters.

"Anne," Joachim said, "our trust in the Lord gives me great pleasure even though we don't understand His intentions. God's plan for our grandson is wondrous, and we are His servants. But I must admit, I don't understand it." Lifting the cup to his lips and sipping the wine, he looked out the window at the gathering darkness. He paused, took a deep breath, and glanced at Anne.

She spoke softly, with a melodic tone. "Our ancestors wrote that the Messiah would spring from the house of David. Our family has prepared over many generations for His coming, but we knew not when nor to whom this blessed gift would occur." She inhaled deeply, paused, and smiled at her husband. "Now our daughter carries the Savior in her womb."

She watched in silence as Joachim rose and walked to the window, where he stared at the gathering stars and the moon. She bit her lip as a single tear coursed down her cheek. Rising from her seat, Anne followed her husband and wrapped her arms around his waist. She shivered as the unknown sent chills down her spine. At the same time, the knowledge of a grandchild being born into their family gave her a sense of humble pride.

"How could this be?" she asked, and then answered herself. "For no other reason than it is the way of the Lord, and we should never question His way."

Joachim turned, took her hands in his, and looked into her eyes. "You speak with knowledge not found in other women. It is His way, not ours. This is a sign of the times to come. The Messiah will not be what many people have thought and prayed for. His coming in this manner is a sign for all to heed. I don't know what the future holds, but it will not be what the Pharisees and Scribes think."

***

Like other young married women, Mary found married life one of excitement and joy but also of new responsibilities. As the child grew in her womb, she suffered morning sickness and pains in her lower back. Nevertheless, unbounded joy filled her heart and soul. She loved His kicking and moving about and thought she could understand His moods even though the child sapped more of her energy with each passing day.

Joseph worked from early light until sunset, tending to the needs of his wife and their unborn child and searching for quality timber for the doors, tables, and benches he built for his customers. The days were not easy, but he never complained.

Nor did Mary, who, filled with happiness, prepared meals, washed clothing, and kept the home tidy and well organized. Their needs were few. When the day drew to a close, they sat in the shade alongside the house on a bench—one of Joseph's finest pieces of work, crafted of rare mahogany wood that came by ship and caravan from across the sea. A nobleman planned to sell the wood at auction but fell upon hard times and traded the lumber to Joseph for work he had already completed.

The mahogany bench became the resting place in the mornings and evenings for the couple. She loved those moments, praying and discussing the future, which they called "the vast unknown." They also spoke of their families, the weather, the crops, and the sheep. More than anything else, they talked about the life of their child, the Son of God. They didn't know why they were chosen, but they committed their faith, lives, and souls without question or hesitation.

The morning broke crisp and clear. Joachim and Anne prepared to sit at the table to complete their morning prayers, then break their fast with a cup of goat milk and a loaf of warm bread made earlier by Rachel.

They were caught off-guard when a child's voice pierced the morning silence. "Master. Master," he cried from beyond the wall surrounding their compound.

"Who is that?" Joachim asked Anne.

"I don't know," she replied as she turned to Rachel. "See who that could be this early in the morning."

As they waited, Joachim ripped a large piece of bread in two, giving one to Anne.

Rachel returned, holding the hand of a little boy of seven or eight years, intense and sinewy of stature, with olive complexion, dark hair, and deep *blue* eyes—obviously not of regional ancestry, yet with a child's Galilean tone of voice. "Master, this child is alone and seeks work so he may earn his keep."

Joachim motioned to the boy, then leaned forward and looked directly into the child's eyes. Speaking firmly but in a comforting tone, he asked, "You want work? You're only a child! Where is your family? Who sent you to me?" Joachim turned quickly and looked at Anne, his tone challenging. "Do you know anything about this?"

Shaking her head, she draped her arm across the boy's shoulders. "Who are you, lad? You're just a child. Where's your family?"

The youngster spoke directly to Joachim. "Sir, I have no family. I traveled here with merchants who allowed me to care for their animals in exchange for safe passage. A woman at the synagogue told me you would give me work. She said you have helped many people." He stood up straight, his shoulders back, and spoke with confidence beyond his age. "I can work. I tended all the animals when we crossed the desert. I washed clothes and helped care for the little children. I drew water and guarded the flocks at night from wild animals."

The boy glanced from Anne to Joachim. "The woman said that each spring you divide your possessions into three equal parts. Your servants take the first portion and deliver it to the poor. They take the second portion to the synagogue for the rabbis and others who work there. You keep the last portion, allowing your flock and crops to yield another harvest which you share the following year. For this reason, she told me you are a man of God, and a person I can trust."

The child stood between Anne and Joachim, glancing from one to the other. "The merchants said it would be better for me to be with a family and not always moving from place to place. You see, sir, that's why she sent me to you. I won't be a burden."

Joachim studied the boy. The early morning sun poured through the window slats, shining on the child's beautiful, black hair. Each strand shone as if spun of fine silk. His eyes were of the deepest blue Joachim had ever seen, surely as deep and clear as the purest well in all of Galilee.

"Give me your foot, child," Joachim said.

He examined the toes and soles carefully, rubbing his hand from toe to heel. The foot manifested calluses yet felt soft and firm. He spat on his fingers and placed them in the boy's armpit and held them there to determine if he had a fever.

He smiled as he spoke to the boy. "You seem to be very well, my little one. Now, tilt your head back." The boy followed his directions as Joachim examined his teeth and gums. "You're a healthy boy, indeed. The merchants took good care of you."

Joachim tousled the boy's hair.

His voice softened. "Sit beside me," he said. "Eat with us now, then Rachel will find you a place to rest. Rachel," he said as the servant returned to the table with bread and milk, "find him garments to wear and sandals for his feet. He can help you here until I determine more about this situation. But for now," he said to the child, "eat and rest. This is your home. If you're going to be with us, then we must call you something. What's your name?"

"Nur, sir. My name is Nur."

"I've heard that name, but never met anyone named Nur," replied Joachim. He nibbled at his lips and frowned. "Nur," he repeated as if to convince himself of the name. "Do you know the meaning of your name, child?'

"Yes, master. It means 'the Light of the Lord.' It's a great name. One that will serve you and your household so long as you allow."

Over the following days, Joachim and Anne gave Nur simple tasks and were amazed at his skill and strength. He helped Rachel with the household chores, went to the fields to tend the sheep and goats, and carried fruit and birds to the temple for the rabbis. In the evenings, he ate dinner with Joachim and Anne, then left their grounds and walked to a nearby hilltop.

Some nights, Joachim followed the youngster into the countryside, where he would go to an outcrop overlooking the valley, sit on a boulder, and stare into the distance. He often looked heavenward, as though mesmerized by the twinkling stars. He sometimes spent hours alone in the darkness before retreating to his quarters near Nadab and Rachel.

"What thoughts pass through that child's mind?" Joachim later asked Anne, telling her what he had seen.

"He's just a child who needs love and guidance," she said. "He is an orphan who needs your strong hand to teach him a skill and your wisdom to teach him the ways of our faith. Why do you think differently?"

"I know only what I see," Joachim said. "He is an unusual child. Very unusual."

Joachim watched as Nur performed his chores—usually as a diligent, capable servant, but from time to time showing a child's carefree attitude. A good boy, he displayed having been well-taught by the merchants or whoever else had been responsible for his upbringing.

Nevertheless, Joachim pondered, this child is a special gift from God.

Before he could decide on the boy's long-term care, Joachim knew he must consult with other leaders. He spent many hours with the rabbis at the synagogue, and even more with his close friend Jonah. Everyone agreed that since the child was an orphan and Joachim an elder, then Joachim should assume responsibility for his rearing.

Joachim also spoke with Sarah, a seamstress in the temple who had found Nur sleeping near the outer wall. She knew a caravan had traveled through the city the day before, so she believed the story the child told her. The caravan traveled from Sidon and Tyre in the north, carrying their wares to the River Jordan and eventually southward toward Jericho and Jerusalem. Vagabonds and an occasional orphan often traveled with merchants, so finding an abandoned child occurred from time to time throughout the merchant season.

Joachim and Anne concluded the will of God had directed the child to seek them out, and it became their responsibility to care for him.

Several weeks after Nur's arrival, Anne told him she would be traveling with Rachel and Nadab to visit her daughter, Mary, and her husband, Joseph. "They live in Nain, nearly a full day's walk from here. Would you like to go with us?"

Nur nodded eagerly.

"Good. We'll leave early tomorrow morning."

Nadab led the donkey loaded with spools of yarn, fresh fruit and bread, water mixed with balsam, and a new mallet for Joseph. Avram, Mary's brother-in-law and the husband of Martha, presented it as a gift for him. Nur followed, leading another ass on which Anne rode. Rachel walked at the rear of the little caravan, occasionally swatting the beast's rump whenever it slowed. However, Nur's diminutive size often prevented him from keeping the stubborn animal from munching weeds along the path.

The morning passed pleasantly. The group stopped only once when Anne called for a rest in the shade of a grove of fig trees. They refreshed themselves and allowed the animals to roll in the dirt and scratch their backs. Nadab and Nur watched the animals, and Anne spoke with Rachel about the upcoming birth of a new grandchild and the attention she would give the child and its parents. Anne treasured her relationship with Rachel, but kept the secret known only to her and to Joachim, Joseph, and Mary. The time would come when the good news of the coming of the Messiah would spread over the land, but until such time as the Lord decreed, each would hold the knowledge in the depths of heart and soul.

The little caravan passed through a dry riverbed and climbed up over the steep bank. In the distance, they could see Mount Precipice, a small but steep fortress-like mountain similar to Masada—a distant place across Samaria and Judea near the Dead Sea.

It amused Anne to watch Nur, an energetic but outmatched youngster being outwitted and outmuscled by the wily jackass. Nur constantly urged the donkey to quicken its dreadfully slow pace, but the diminutive little beast moved at her own pace. The harder Nur pulled, the more the young mare stiffened her resolve to take her time. The little jenny refused to go any faster than her own plodding pace.

Anne exchanged glances with Rachel, and they burst out with laughter at the child's frustration. In a final effort, Anne took hold of the cord and, with a slight jerk, pulled it from Nur's hand. "Run on," she said, waving her hand. "Go tell them we're coming."

Nur smiled and nodded, then broke into a dead run. He passed Nadab and the other donkey as he shouted over his shoulder, "I'll have water for you when you get there."

He rounded a curve in the path, through a grove of palm trees, and up the last few steps of the hill to the rock wall surrounding the home of Mary, Joseph, and their unborn child, the Son of God, the King of Kings.

When Nur reached the wall, he saw Joseph stepping outside the house. Joseph appeared to be about the same age as Nadab. His physical stature surprised Nur—much taller and broader in the shoulders than how he perceived him from Anne's description. His curly, dark brown hair hung to his shoulders and blended in with a full beard that covered his face.

"Ho, lad," Joseph shouted as he trotted down the path toward Nur. Reaching him, he grasped the child around the waist and hoisted him to his shoulder. "News of your stay with Anne and Joachim has spread quickly, and what I heard is true. You are indeed a good-looking boy." Joseph lowered him to the ground and draped his arm over Nur's shoulder. "Welcome to our home, young man."

"Thank you, sir," Nur replied as he wrapped his arms around Joseph's waist. "Thank you very much."

"Why don't you fetch a jug of water from the spring behind the house?" Joseph suggested. "It will be refreshing to them after their long journey."

Nur obeyed immediately and dashed to the spring, filled an earthen jug, and just as quickly ran to the front of the house.

"I'm back," he shouted. His eyes followed Joseph's gaze to Mary as she came outside. Nur's breath caught in his throat when he looked upon her elegant, innocent beauty.

Not being mindful of where he put his feet, Nur stumbled and nearly dropped the water jug. He steadied himself, then handed it to Joseph, whose eyes were still on Mary.

Her resplendent beauty awed the youngster. She stood a full head taller than Nur but considerably shorter than her husband. She wore a blue gown the shade of a robin's egg with a golden-colored trim around the hem. A white mantle covered her head and draped down to her waist. It, too, was trimmed with golden threads. Her cheeks glowed with a joyful expression. Her soft lips curved into a smile, but when she spoke, her clear and musical voice resonated like a joyful hymn.

She stood in the doorway, smiled at Nur, then reached out her hand in welcome. "Greetings and peace, my friend," she said.

"Peace to you, my lady," he replied.

Taking Nur's hand and carrying the water jug in the other, Joseph led them down the path toward the grove to meet the others.

Even as they walked, Nur could not stop looking over his shoulder at Mary, a model of beauty and purity.

They had nearly reached the grove when Nadab appeared, followed by the others. Anne slid off the jenny and ran the last few steps to her son-in-law, greeting him with a kiss on each cheek. She sipped the cold, refreshing water, then shared it with Nur, Rachel, and Nadab. After whetting their thirst, Nadab and Rachel led the animals while Anne walked beside Joseph and Nur to the wall.

Spotting Mary, and with tears in her eyes, Anne lifted her hem and raced up the path to the front step where she hugged and kissed her daughter.

Nur followed Joseph, Nadab, and Rachel to a shallow cave that served as a stable. Here, they unloaded their belongings and tended the animals.

Glancing at Nur, Joseph commented, "You, my friend, will spend the night in the house with us. I have prepared for you a blanket behind the screen where you can rest, but you will be near enough if you need us, or," he smiled, "if we need you."

After completing their tasks, Joseph and Nur entered the house to find Anne and Mary deep in conversion. They were seated on a couch sharing a cup of juice as they talked. Nur stopped in his tracks. Their conversation remained hushed, but the tension in their faces manifested the seriousness of whatever they were discussing.

"What is it?" Joseph asked. "Did you already tell her before they had time to rest?"

"Yes," Mary said. "It's too important. I had to tell her. I didn't want to worry her but had to share this news with my mother."

Anne interjected. "Come talk to me, Joseph." Pulling a folded blanket from the end of the couch, she spread it on the floor at their feet. "Sit with us and tell me this story."

Joseph lowered himself to the floor and crossed his legs. "This very morning a soldier from Nazareth came through. He delivered a message for all of us. Every citizen must return immediately to his homeland and be counted for a census." He placed his hand on Mary's bare foot. "That means my wife must accompany me. We both must go." Looking up at Anne, he continued, "I tried to explain to the soldier about my wife's condition, but he said the census has been ordered by Cyrenius, so there are no alternatives. We must go."

Anne gave a soft laugh when she spoke. "Then, that is why God sent us to you at this time. We're here to help you, can you not see?" She leaned over and put her hands on Joseph's shoulders. "Let Rachel go with you. They will never know the difference, and your wife can stay here. We will care for her." She looked at her daughter. "You cannot travel, Mary. Do you understand that? You must not go. The time for the child is at hand."

Mary put her arms around her mother and held her tightly. "Oh, Mother, if it were only that simple." She turned to Nur, who sat on the floor close to the door. "Please, Nur, go see if Rachel needs help. We'll call you if we need you."

Mary stood up. "Please, Mother, put your hands on my stomach. Feel the child inside me. Feel the Lamb of God. We cannot let Him come into the world while we bear false witness, even if it is to a Roman. We cannot lie." Leaning forward, she kissed her mother's forehead. "I know of your love for all of us, and that you want only what's right for God in heaven, but this must be."

"I, too, have an idea," Joseph said as he walked to the door, calling for Nur. "Nur, come talk with us."

Nur raced into the house where Joseph motioned him onto the blanket.

"In the best of times, it's about an eight-day trip from here to Bethlehem." Joseph paused. "Indeed, Mother, the Lord God sent you to us because it will be a hard journey, but your being here has made it easier for us. Let Nur go with us. He has proven to be an able worker, has he not?

Mother, lend us one of your donkeys, and with the one we own, we'll be able to travel with reasonable comfort and speed. I'll pack one with our goods for the journey, and the other I'll prepare for Mary to ride."

He gazed at Mary with his eyes smiling and sparkling. "I'll make you comfortable, or at least as comfortable as you can be with child. This boy shall become a man and help us. We know the way is fraught with robbers and highwaymen, but Nur can run ahead of us and warn us of danger. Mother, with your blessings, your animal, and this strong young man to help, we'll have a safe and good journey."

"Oh, please," Nur begged. "I'll be a big help to them. I give you my word."

"I know you will, child," Anne said as she kissed the boy's cheek. She turned to Joseph, nodded her approval, then took her daughter with the unborn child into her arms. She whispered softly into her daughter's ear, "Be careful, my child, and may the glory of God go with you."

Chapter Two
The Census

Dawn broke brilliantly over the rocky hills of Galilee and Samaria, casting its piercing rays across the desert floor, beyond the Plain of Esdraelon, lighting the house of Joseph and Mary and their guests. With the first crow of the rooster, Joseph rose and began to pack the animals for the trip.

The rising sun caressed Mary's face. She rolled over and turned her back, giving herself a few more moments of rest. From the chatter and clatter of the household, she knew Anne had risen also, so she sat up, put on her sandals, wrapped a mantle around her head and shoulders, and prepared herself for the day.

Mary completed her ablutions, then roused Nur, who slept beneath the blanket she had given him. Rachel and Nadab joined them for a breakfast of bread, fresh milk, and fruit from Joseph's ample grove of date and apricot trees. Joseph led them in prayer, seeking the Lord's blessings on their food and asking for strength and guidance for the journey they were about to undertake. They ate in silence, each nurturing their private thoughts.

As a youngster is prone to do, Nur finished first then, at Joseph's direction, went to the spring to fill the remainder of the waterskins they would carry with them. Joseph and Nadab left the table to begin the final arrangements of fitting the donkeys for the trip.

Rachel looked about, then busied herself cleaning the house.

When Anne and Mary were alone, Anne began to weep.

"Don't cry, Mother," Mary pleaded. "Please, I don't understand why the Romans insist that each member of the household shall appear in person for the census, especially when a woman is pregnant, but I have faith the Lord will provide for whatever hardships we will face." Mary, too, wept, then reached for her mother's hands, which she kissed. "Have faith in God Almighty. He has sent His child to us, and whatever we encounter we'll overcome with His help. It is very simple, but also hard to understand. The prophecy is fulfilled. From Abraham to Isaac and throughout history, our people have awaited God's covenant. Now it is here." She looked upon her husband as tears of joy flowed over her cheeks. "And we have been chosen."

When the animals were loaded, Nur took Joseph's hand and led him to the side of the house. "Sir," Nur said.

Joseph responded quickly, "Do not call me sir. From this day forward, I will be your father. You'll go with us wherever we go, do whatever we do, and remain with us forever." He put his hands on the boy's shoulders. "From this moment on, you are our child. I will teach you my trade and raise you as if you were our own."

"Thank you, sir. I mean, Father." Nur stood tall and proud, his heart nearly bursting with joy. "But I must tell you something important."

"What is it, child? Tell me."

"In my sleep, a young man came to me and spoke. I told him I had to sleep and to leave me alone. A second time he came to me, and again I told him to leave me alone. A third time he came to me and told me not to speak but to listen."

"And?" Joseph asked.

"The man said he brought us a message from his Father, and we must put our trust in Him for this journey. As you have said, the way is dangerous with the threat of robbers and other evil men. But, if we follow where the new donkey leads, we'll be in safe hands. If the baby is to be brought unharmed into the land of our people, you must follow the way of the new animal," Nur said as he pointed to the donkey Anne had given to them. "That animal knows the way."

"Speak, child," Joseph roared. "What are you saying?"

Nur looked into Joseph's eyes. "Father, I know only what is commanded by the Father in heaven because it is He who sent a messenger in the night.

Why me? I do not know. I only know what is, and this is the message from the one who came to me in the night."

"You confuse me, child," Joseph snapped. He walked away from Nur and sat on the wall surrounding their home. "What am I supposed to do? Why is this happening to us now?"

Nur followed and climbed up on the wall beside his father. "I mean you no ill will or harm. I mean only to be your servant, and I bring you the message that I received. Nothing other than that."

Joseph draped his arm around his son's shoulders and held him tightly, contemplating the recent events: the soldier with the message, the arrival of Anne and Nur, Nur's dream, and now his message about the donkey.

Joseph struggled to comprehend it—so much happened so quickly. With Mary's delivery coming in a few days, what else could God give him to consider? Though neither lazy nor fearful, but how much more should he have to endure? And now this child named Nur telling him of the dream and of their need to follow the dumb animal, to allow it to lead them to Bethlehem, and Nur speaking of the coming child. *How much more awaits us?* he wondered.

The sun climbed high above the horizon before they began the journey. Anne would remain with Rachel and Nadab for a few days until they could arrange for someone to look after the house, the groves, and the animals; then, they would return to Nazareth.

Nur mounted the ass Anne had given to them, but the little beast was free of the bridle and able to move freely in any direction.

Following behind Nur and the donkey, Joseph led the second animal on whose back Mary rode sidesaddle, her left leg dangling close to the ground. She draped her right leg around the knot of the leather belt tied around the animal's girth. Each of the donkeys carried a few belongings, as the family wanted to move swiftly.

The tiny caravan moved south toward Nain, then followed a well-traveled trail into the vast, open desert. Nur sat comfortably on the ass, occasionally looking back. Mary had scooted around to a more secure position. She appeared comfortable despite her large stomach and the animal's lurching gait. She smiled at Nur and nodded her approval of his leadership. They were off to a good start.

Soon they passed Mount Moriah, and by late afternoon they reached the cool Springs of Harod. Here they could camp beneath the trees and find safety in the numbers of pilgrims who stopped at this site once used by Gideon and his thousands of soldiers.

A false dawn painted a faint glow on the morning of the second day. Joseph opened his eyes, yawned, and slipped from beneath his fleece blanket. He shuddered when his bare feet touched the hard and cold desert floor, grasping the blanket and holding it close to his face. Though no rain had fallen for many weeks, he smelled fresh dew that soaked his blanket. He understood the message—identical to that when Gideon received his communication from God. Joseph bowed his head in silent prayer, giving thanks to God and pledging his faith to persevere against any powers they might face.

After a meal of bread and fruit, the family moved out with the other travelers who headed north and south toward their fathers' homes for the census. Nur's ass followed the trail toward the Jezreel Valley, plodding over the ruts and stones in the roadway, leading them toward Bethlehem. They traveled only a short distance before the animal turned west and climbed up a dry ravine away from the highway the other travelers used.

The donkey began a gradual climb toward distant hills until they were out of sight of the road. "Nur, what are you doing?" Joseph shouted. "Pull him back! He's going the wrong way!"

Leaving Mary, Joseph ran to the lead animal, intending to guide him back to the road. When he reached for the animal's ear, Nur put his hand on Joseph's. "No, Father, please."

Joseph released his grip and looked first at Nur, then at Mary, who sat on the back of the other donkey. In her melodic and soothing tone, she spoke. "The child possesses wisdom we do not yet understand. We must have faith in God."

Joseph shook his head and wiped his brow with the back of his hand. His words were soft but surrendering. "I understand."

And so, the days passed. Instead of following the road across Samaria and on to Bethlehem, they rode far to the west, following the animal as it led them across steep, rocky mountains and barren deserts. They traveled far into the wilderness toward the Great Sea before turning south. At each day's end, they found a place with fresh, cool water where trees protected them from the burning rays of the sun and the winds that swept across the vast openness.

During the journey, Joseph worried about the day Mary would deliver her child and where they'd be. They were alone in a strange land, following an animal and a child. The trip should have taken them directly south, where they could find lodging and fresh food in Beth Shan and the other towns along the valleys of the River Jordan, but instead, they found themselves isolated.

Five days passed, each one ending with the family encamped in the bleak desert, their meager supplies dwindling. Nevertheless, the donkey invariably led them to water where they could refresh themselves and wash the grime from their bodies.

Anxious and nervous, Joseph assumed the child would come before they returned home. With that worry heavy on his heart, he feared they would be unable to find a midwife. Would he be able to help her deliver safely? Though concerned about the challenges ahead, he placed his and all of their lives in the hands of God.

Young Nur developed a sense of vigilance over his newfound patriarch. "Father, I shall travel ahead of you and your wife and be watchful, always mindful of my duty. I know your heart is heavy, and I pray to God. Be at peace. When her time arrives, wherever we are, He will provide."

Alert but confident, Nur smiled inwardly when they rolled into their fleece blankets.

His mother whispered into his ear while she pulled her blanket to her chin, "Peace be with you, Nur." Ever mindful of her beloved husband, she looked at Joseph and placed her hand on his brow. "And peace to you, my good and loving husband. The Lord God requires you to understand the strength of our faith in Him, and He finds us strong."

She shivered and pulled her blanket over her face for protection from the night breeze that swept in from the sea.

"Peace be to you," Joseph replied, moving closer to protect her from the wind.

On the sixth day, Nur's donkey turned away from the sea and began a gradual ascent up the hills. They rested at midday after cresting a bleak rocky outcrop where a single eucalyptus tree grew between the boulders and the hard desert floor. Joseph meted out the last of their water between the three of them and the two donkeys. Mary sat on the ground. She leaned against the tree as Joseph and Nur walked to the top of the next hill. In the distance, Joseph spied the town of Emmaus, a place he had often visited.

"Mary," he shouted, "Emmaus. We'll be there for the night!"

He grabbed Nur's hand, ran down the side of the hill, jumped a ditch at the bottom, and raced back to the tree where Mary rested.

Nur slowed as they neared Mary, allowing his father to share the good news privately. At long last, they would have shelter, food, and a decent rest before they set out on the remainder of their journey. He heard them laughing and talking when he approached the shade of the tree. It pleased him because, once again, God Almighty blessed them to face their journey's travail.

Joseph took Mary's hand and helped her rise to her feet. Nur jumped on the back of his faithful little beast, and Joseph helped Mary onto the back of her donkey. Joseph grinned broader than he had done for many days. "Let me tell you, I've been to Emmaus many times on business, and I know the people there. Yes, tonight will be a rich reward for this trip."

He patted the animals' rumps to speed them up and had to trot to stay up with them as they plodded and slid down one hill, then grunted and hopped up the next. They had survived the worst of the trip. Should Mary deliver here, there would be many friends to help.

Nightfall approached when they entered the city, walking past the few houses on the outskirts of the town. "I know where we'll go," said Joseph. "My friend Seth has bought many things from me, always at a fair price. You will meet my friends tonight, and when we leave tomorrow, we will travel fresh and clean."

"I am glad, too," said Nur.

"I, too," Mary said, "am more than glad not to spend another night on the hard ground." She smiled the most precious of smiles at Nur and her husband. "I am blessed to be with you, wherever we are."

"And we with you, my mother," Nur replied.

His donkey lifted its head and inhaled deeply. At the scent of water, it began a slow trot. As they approached the center of the city, Joseph directed them to the home of his friend, Seth. They stopped at the well, and Nur jumped from the back of the donkey and began lowering jugs for water.

"Wait here while I speak to Seth," Joseph said. He walked with a bouncing gait through the compound's entry to greet his friend.

Meanwhile, Mary slipped from the back of the animal and sat on a bench alongside the well. She wrapped her mantle tightly around her as the cool breeze brushed against her shoulders.

"Are you cold, Mother?" Nur asked as he gave her a water jug.

"No, but I am relieved to be here," she replied.

Nur sat on the ground at her feet, putting his arms around her knees and holding her close. "Me, too," he whispered, then pulled his tunic tightly around him against the chill of the evening breeze. He looked into her eyes and spoke in a manner not that of a child. "Thank you, Mother, for caring for me. I will always be here to serve and repay you for your kindness."

"Someday, Nur, you will be a grown man like my husband, and you will take a wife of your own and have children."

"No, Mother, that is not to be." He looked again into her eyes. His young face manifested knowledge beyond his years. "That is not to be."

They sat for a long moment looking at each other until Nur broke the silence.

"You will bear a great child who will bring you joy and happiness, but you will be pierced by a thorn. You will grieve. But I will stand beside you when your heart is heavy as no other does."

"Do you understand what you say, child?" Mary asked.

Nur nodded. "I will be your flame, lighting your lamp and fire to warm your home. When all others have left you, there I will be." Nur took Mary's hands in his own. "Today I am a child, but I will care for you until the end of time." He leaned forward and lifted himself to her, then kissed her cheek.

Nur and Mary watched the gathering darkness sweep across the land. Joseph had been gone too long. Finally, Nur stood and walked several steps away, gazing at the first stars in the eastern sky.

"Look, Mother," he said. He pointed his outstretched arm toward the distant stars. "When traveling with the merchants, I heard them conversing with astrologers from the East, and they spoke of the strange alignment of the stars. Look," he said again.

Mary stepped beside him and gazed into the vast sky above. She saw stars where she had never seen them before in places they had never been. "Tell me of this strange thing," she said quizzically.

"They were men from far away, but they followed the stars into our land where they could see them clearly. They used words new to me, but they spoke something about the joining together of stars in the sky." He looked at her, then back at the sky. "Some say when the stars are like this, they have joined together and are one new star. But the astrologers are wise men, saying it is not one, but three that appear as one. Whatever it is, it is very unusual."

"Indeed, it is," she replied as she looked into the eastern sky and the stars that appeared as one. "Very unusual."

Chapter Three
The Nativity

They returned to the bench and took up their wait. Shortly, Joseph returned with his head bowed, shuffling his feet. He carried a cloth holding several pieces of fruit, a few loaves of bread, and several fish.

"There is no room for us," he said. "The census brought all my friends and their families here." He shrugged his shoulders and forced a smile. "They shared their food with us, and we can fill our waterskins from the well."

Holding herself erect and poised, Mary spoke in a soft and enduring tone. "But, Joseph, they are your friends, and our child's birth is near. Did you tell them?"

Joseph showed his frustration, his voice tense, his brow furrowed as he answered. "There is no room for us. None, anywhere." He pointed to the hills in the west. "Up there," they said. "That's where we will find shelter beneath the trees." He gently lay the palm of his hand on her stomach. "They'll send a midwife if we need one. That is all anyone can do."

They quickly filled their jugs as the cold wind swept forcefully across the land. Seeing Mary shiver, Nur placed his mantle around her shoulders. Together, he and Joseph helped her onto the donkey, and they rode away from Emmaus into the hills. They rode only a short distance before entering a small grove where massive boulders protected them from the wind. The lead donkey stopped, shook its head, and stomped its hooves into the dirt. It had delivered them to where they would set up the camp for the night.

After completing the meal, Joseph told them about the news from his friend, Seth. Their journey far to the east from the usual route proved to be a guidance sign from God. Robbers had attacked many travelers, killing, looting, and raping. If they had journeyed on the main highway, they, too, might have fallen into the hands of the evil ones. The donkey had led them to safety over the mountains. It always found fresh water and delivered them to Emmaus where they could replenish their food for a few days. Instead of being saddened by the long roundabout trip and failing to find lodging in Emmaus, they joined in a prayer of thanksgiving.

Once again, Joseph spread the blankets on the ground. The breeze increased, adding to the chill of the night air. Joseph placed Nur beneath a blanket between him and Mary to protect the child from the weather. The donkeys rolled in the dirt, scratching their backs and enjoying freedom from their burdens. Then, they lay by Mary and Joseph, shielding them from the wind.

On the seventh, eighth, and ninth days, the donkey led them along an indirect route toward Eshtaol and Beth Shemesh, but they could not find lodging anywhere.

"All of our family is here. We have no room for you. Go away!" They heard those words each day for three days. Each late afternoon, Joseph and Nur set up their modest camp at the head of a spring or alongside a small pool of water in the rocks. They slept beneath their blankets with the animals sharing their bodies' warmth.

Joseph beamed when they reached the outskirts of Bethlehem at the end of the tenth day of their travels. "Thank God, we are here," he said to no one in particular. "Thank God." He shouted to Nur, who had moved ahead, "Nur, wait for us. I know where we'll go. They'll receive us with open arms." He looked at Mary and smiled. "You did it. Here you can rest, and when your time comes, my friends will send a midwife to deliver the child."

"Stop the donkey," Mary said. "I want to walk the remaining distance. I feel so good." With Nadab holding her hand, she slipped down from the donkey. Taking a deep breath and standing tall, a refreshing burst of energy flowed through her body. Relaxed but eager to move along, she rearranged the mantle over her head so that it would fit snugly over her hair, around her shoulders, and flow down her arms. The soft white of the veil blended with the delicate blue of her dress, its hem touching the ground. She walked several steps behind Joseph until they caught up to Nur.

"We're here, and all is well," said Nur, who also dismounted.

Mary strolled behind them, proudly watching Joseph and Nur leading the way into the city. Throughout the arduous trip, her husband and child found food and water, protected her from the cold, and looked after her comfort. With her heart filled with love, she knew they would be there when the Son of God came into the world. She felt no worry or anxiety, only peace and happiness about the coming birth of the Messiah.

Entering the city streets, Nur turned to Joseph. "Tell me, Father, you know many of these people, do you not?"

"Oh, yes, I trust them to give us shelter and allow us to find a home where we can live during the census and while we pay the tax." Joseph handed the donkey's reins to Nur and directed him to a well where he and Mary could rest while Joseph arranged for lodging.

Happy to be of service, Nur gladly held the reins in one hand and Mary's hand in his other. They walked only a short distance where they could rest in the shade of a pavilion. He placed a blanket on a bench for Mary, helped her off the donkey, and gave her a cup of water. Then he poured water into a shallow dish, removed Mary's sandals, washed and dried her feet with his tunic, and placed her sandals back on her feet.

She laid her hand on his shoulder and pulled him to her. "You are a blessed child."

"Blessed are you and the child you are about to bring forth," he replied.

"Who are you, Nur?" Mary asked. "One so full of wisdom."

His voice soft but profound, Nur looked deeply into her eyes. "I am an orphan sent to serve and be with you when you need me most. I learned from the merchants and others who sometimes traveled with them that we should serve each other, not ourselves."

He twisted about, then made himself comfortable on the ground at her feet. "I'm a child and sometimes want to play with others, and sometimes do, but my life and yours are very much alike." He smiled and tossed a pebble at a stray cat stalking a bird pecking in the dirt. "We can love ourselves and each other and still play, can we not?"

"Nur, sometimes your understanding is too much for me," Mary said. "But yes, I think you are quite right."

The warmth of the afternoon sun overtook Nur. Crawling onto the bench, he laid his head on Mary's lap, felt the movement of the unborn child, smiled, and drifted off into a well-deserved nap. Mary rested her head on the back of the bench and slept, feeling Nur's warmth against her, listening to his breathing, and imagining the mystery that lay ahead.

Joseph returned late in the day and found them still asleep. He hesitated, then touched Mary's shoulder. "We need to go," he said. His voice was somber; his expression echoed the deep hollowness of his heart.

Nur roused, rubbed his eyes, and stretched. He slowly rose to his feet. His voice soft but inquisitive, he asked, "Where are we going, Father?"

"Up there." Joseph pointed toward the hills. "Everything and every place is full." He looked at his little family. "I'm sorry. I thought I knew so many people and they would gladly take us in, or at least know a safe place where we could stay." He shook his head, bit his lip, and continued, "But that is not the case. I am sorry for you," he said to Mary. "Sorry that I led you to believe I knew so many people and that everything here would be well. I've been everywhere. There is nothing."

"Where will we go?" she asked.

"Up there." Joseph pointed toward the hills again. "It is not far. We'll do our best with whatever we find." He helped Mary to her feet, her size so great that she found it more challenging to move with each passing day. "Nur, bring the jenny," he said.

"No," Mary uttered. "I cannot get back on that poor little creature." She gave a halfhearted laugh.

The family followed an animal trail and walked into the barren hills. "Only a little farther," Joseph said, pointing to a rocky hillside where they could see the entrance to several small caves. "My friend Cosam keeps his animals there, and we can share it. We'll be out of the wind and the night air. Nur and I will make it clean and ready for the baby."

After a strenuous climb for Mary, they reached a plateau where three caves faced out toward Bethlehem. A barricade of stones and timbers enclosed each entrance so the cattle, donkeys, and a few sheep could move freely in and out of the cave but could not wander away. Joseph looked first in one, then in the second, and finally in the third before he decided the middle cave would best suit their needs.

Under his father's direction, Nur moved the animals out of the cave and into the fenced area while Joseph cleaned out old silage and animal waste. He piled animal chips, sticks, and a broken piece of lumber near the entrance. Then he placed a bit of oil beneath the sticks, and in a few minutes, the flicker of a flame glowed. It gradually warmed the rocks and heated the cave. He sent Nur to find grass and wildflowers to freshen the dank odor of the cave where the Son of God would come into the world.

Nur ran toward the gully at the bottom of the hill and followed it to a spring that dripped a trickle of water where wild grasses and flowers grew. He removed the wrap from his shoulders and gathered a few plants—dandelions and anemones, as well as chicory and watercress, then ran as fast as his feet would carry him back to the cave.

He found Mary wrapped in her blanket, lying close to the fire.

Joseph took the plants and flowers and divided them into two piles. The first he crushed and put into a clay pot filled with water. He placed the pot against the glowing embers, and a sweet aroma rose with the steam, overwhelming the smell of the animals. He divided the others into two bouquets, placing one on the ground at Mary's shoulders and the other cupped in her hands.

Her eyes pierced Joseph's heart. "Thank you, my love." She smiled at him and then turned to Nur. "Thank you, my sweet child. I appreciate your help. Truly, you are the flame of the Lord, and we could not do without you." She plucked a flower from her little bouquet and handed it to him. "Thank you, Nur. For you truly are the Light of the Lord."

As Mary slept, Joseph prepared a meal of dried fish and bread and broke open a pomegranate. He spread the remaining blankets on the ground next to Mary, laid out the meal, and then woke her. She had little appetite, but Joseph and Nur consumed everything Joseph prepared.

When they finished their meal, Mary reached for Joseph's hand and whispered, "The time has come."

Nur wiped the sweat from her brow with his mantel.

She bit her lower lip and held it tightly between her teeth. "The time is here," she said again.

Joseph jumped to his feet. He took Nur by the hand and led him outside. "Look there," he said, pointing to a distant house. "That is where Cosam lives. Run there and bring the midwife."

As soon as he spoke, a warm breeze swept up the valley. In the heavens, the clouds roiled and tumbled. Lightning and thunder filled the sky. Joseph's skin tingled. His heart pounded, his breath grew short as the wind and thunder roared, and lightning filled the night's blackness. He fell to his knees, sensing Nur beside him. They humbled themselves and lay prostrate in the dirt and manure of the stable yard. The sounds of the angels and archangels, cherubim and seraphim, and all the heavenly hosts filled the heavens, singing of the wonder and glory of Almighty God and His newborn Son. The clouds parted, and the stars shone brightly above Bethlehem and the faraway lands, casting a vivid hue over the hill, as though a new sun rose in the night. The wind subsided, and a peaceful quiet settled over the countryside.

Joseph and Nur stood, their garments shining white and covered with gold dust that reflected the night's light. Joseph looked toward the cave, nearly blinded by the light of a thousand suns emanating from within. Nur and Joseph entered the cave together, shielding their eyes with their hands. The smell of roses filled the air, and the light dimmed until only a glow settled over a manger filled with straw where the Virgin had placed the Christ child.

Mary sat alongside the manger and arranged a clean white cloth around the baby. She looked at Nur and Joseph. Her face shone with God's blessing of peace and joy. "He's here. Our family is complete. Now we must give praise and glory to God."

Joseph and Nur prostrated themselves again to pay homage to the King of Kings. The child whimpered and began to cry. Joseph rose, lifting Him from His crib, and held Him close, rocking and speaking softly to Him. But the little one had other thoughts, so Joseph gave Him to His mother. He and Nur left them alone for the Son of God to partake of His mother's gift.

As Nur sat on the stable fence, he heard voices and the sounds of men approaching. "Father," he said in a loud whisper. "Someone is coming. Is there anything I should do?"

"No," Joseph replied. "I see them. Look there." He pointed toward the opposite hill. "They're shepherds. They must have seen the brilliance of the sky and heard the heavenly sounds in the valley at Beit Sahour. They are coming to adore the child." Joseph glanced at Nur. "My child, you know, do you not?"

"I do, my father. I do. He is the Christ, come to redeem the world."

Nur climbed down from the fence surrounding the stable and stood beside Joseph. They watched in silence at the approaching shepherds.

Then, Nur spoke. "He is the Messiah, born of the poor to lead all people to His Father in heaven."

Chapter Four
The Magi

After paying homage to the child, the shepherds returned to their families and friends and told them of the glory and splendor they had witnessed. As though scattered by the desert wind, word of the magnificent event spread throughout the land.

The days following the birth of the baby were filled with excitement. Birds soared on the gentle breezes that carried the scent of freshly budding flowers across the hillsides. Young lambs bounced around each other while their mothers basked in the warm afternoon sun. All were at peace.

Many people followed the shepherds' footsteps and came to pay tribute to the baby and His family. Most of the visitors were shepherds and other laborers of the fields, poor in material possessions but rich in faith. Also, some people of wealth heard and believed.

All the visitors to the cave on the hillside brought gifts for the Holy Family. Some brought only a slender shoot of a budding flower; some brought turtledoves; others brought fruit and clothing for the child. From the wealthier visitors, the gifts included fine linen and delicate oils. In a few cases, they presented silver shekels minted in Tyre.

All gave generously within their means from wherever or no matter how far they traveled. The little family accepted each gift, whether large or small, as an honor bestowed upon the Child of God.

Nur gave witness to all of this. While Joseph and Mary attended to the child's needs and received their guests, Nur busied himself with caring for their humble dwelling. He and Joseph made screens from the pieces of linen, dividing the cave into partitions to separate their sleeping quarters from where they conducted their other daily activities.

All the while, he watched and learned from the visitors. Many of them were poor and had nothing tangible to give. Nevertheless, they offered their adoration to the child in the manger.

Some visitors were men of ebony skin who provided protection to their masters from bandits or other men who their masters considered undesirable. These strong, handsome men came to justify their souls. Still others were compassionate women whose hearts went out to the young woman who gave birth without the aid of a midwife.

Whatever their background or social status, each person came to bear witness and give of themselves to this child.

Nur cared for the infant in the evenings after the visitors had gone and the family could relax and enjoy each other's company in solitude and prayer. He washed the baby's face, put oil on His tiny body, and used clean fabrics to brush Jesus' dark, curly hair back. He swaddled the baby in linen each night before placing Him in the crib for a short sleep before His appetite roused Him.

To Nur, being in the cave represented an abundance of wealth as he found a life embraced by love and the grace of God. He could not ask for more. This sanctuary provided much more than simply a cave or stable. It manifested more earthly elegance than Judea's most refined and powerful kingdom or anywhere in the Roman Empire. Indeed, this cave and stable exceeded elegance far beyond the wealthiest place in all the land.

Joseph and Nur prepared their dwelling for the circumcision that would take place on the eighth day after the birth. Choosing from the linens and rugs they had received, they repurposed several timbers from the fences and constructed a diminutive *pergola,* a projecting eave extending out from the cave's entrance.

They paid close attention to the smallest detail as they went about their duties. They spaced the poles upright, hanging the linens to shade the ground beneath it, and laid the rugs in the shade.

Alongside the pergola, Nur built a fire pit where they would prepare a meal for the priests who would perform the ceremony and the visitors and other guests in attendance. Upon completing their task, they stood with hands on hips, confident that when the time arrived, the celebration of the holy rite would occur with the grace and dignity it deserved.

Under Mary's guiding eye, they sorted through the gifts to give to the poor who had nothing to offer, and so began His service to the world.

Nur stayed with his mother and brother on the evening of the seventh day while Joseph walked to the city to summon the priests. When they returned, an elegant banquet awaited them beneath the pavilion. Mary and Nur prepared enough food for themselves, the priests, and the guests who may come to witness the holy event. By tradition, the poor of the city followed the priests so they could observe the rite and participate in the banquet.

By nightfall, many gathered to enjoy the food and drink. After completing the meal, the priest began a repetitious chant and song, praying for the blessings of the Most High to descend upon this child. The religious rite continued into the night, and the guests found places to rest. Nur tended the fire and helped Joseph, his friends, and their wives clean the pavilion and dwelling before he, too, slipped behind his screen and fell asleep.

The eighth day dawned with a sky as lustrous and blue as the world had ever witnessed. The first glow of sunlight swept the hillside, rousing the visitors and washing away the early morning chill.

Joseph and Nur served cheese and bread to those who had gathered from near and far for the ceremony. Then, each person made themselves reasonably comfortable in the stable yard to witness the holy rite. Joseph seated the three priests with their backs to the cave entrance so they were facing the rising sun. He placed before them a stone slab they carried from the city. Atop it, Joseph laid the sheath and knife of circumcision. With everything in place, he took a position beside the priest and nodded to Nur to bring Mary and the child to the ceremony.

A pair of cooing doves on the hillside broke the silence, their delicate perch swaying in the morning breeze.

Nur and Mary came from the cave with the newborn nestled in His mother's arms. Mary stood elegant and graceful, manifesting the holiness of the mother of the Son of God. A white mantle trimmed in golden threads covered all but a wisp of hair. Her blue gown enveloped all but the tips of her fingers and toes.

Jesus' precious face and dark eyes shone bright and clear. Swaddled in fresh white linen, His hair dark and curly, the Son of God had come to fulfill the Law and the Prophets.

Nur stepped around the four men and stood with his back to the sun, casting his shadow across the slab and the sheath, the knife still safely in place. Mary followed him through the entrance and handed the child to Joseph, who presented Him to the priest who stood between his companions.

The priest took the child in his arms, breathed on His face, then presented the child to the world with outstretched arms toward the rising sun. Nur watched in silence as the priest held the child aloft and hummed softly under his breath, turning to the north, the south, the west, and finally back to the east. When everyone had the opportunity to see the baby, the priest placed the child on the slab beside the sheathed knife.

Nur watched, breathless, as the second priest removed the cloth from the child while the third priest raised the sheath to the rising sun and slid the sharpened stone blade out. He held it high overhead, reflecting the sunlight off the polished stone.

The naked baby lay atop His swaddling clothes. In a swift, measured motion, the first priest took the knife and completed the circumcision. The child gave a piercing cry. Tears filled Mary's eyes as she quickly scooped Him into her arms. Without hesitation, she bathed Him in oil and placed a juice-sweetened cloth to His lips. The child responded, sucking on the fabric as the oils deadened His pain. The chief priest took the baby from His mother, lifted the child for all to see, then wrapped the baby tightly into a clean cloth and returned Him to Joseph.

"What is the child's name?" asked the priest.

"Jesus," replied Joseph. "His name is Jesus." Joseph kissed the baby's forehead, then gave the child to His mother who walked among the visitors so they could see Him. Then she returned to the three priests and held the child in her outstretched arms. Each priest nodded in approval of the baby boy and His name.

The chief priest spoke loudly so all could hear. "This child shall be called Jesus."

The visitors cheered and quickly ate and drank the food and wine from the previous evening's meal. Nur ensured that everyone had enough, then helped Joseph distribute gifts to everyone as they prepared to leave.

The next several days passed uneventfully, with Joseph and Nur keeping the cave clean while Mary tended to Jesus. On the afternoon of the fifteenth day, Anne and Joachim arrived, having been summoned by a messenger sent by Cosam to tell them the news. Traveling with the grandparents, Rachel, Nadab, and a contingent of servants and animals carried enough goods to satisfy their needs for a considerable period.

While Mary and Joseph greeted her parents, Nur helped Nadab unload the packs from the animals. Rachel and the other servants found quarters in the nearby caves. They cleaned the camps and prepared an evening meal before the sun faded.

Joachim and Anne beamed as more visitors took turns holding and caressing their beautiful grandchild. Indeed, the joyful evening exceeded all their expectations.

Night fell before Nur had an opportunity to hold the baby in his lap. The others watched with interest as they became aware of the unique relationship between Nur and the child. The baby stared into Nur's eyes without blinking, and Nur breathed softly on Jesus' face. Neither made a sound, yet something passed between the two children.

Joachim observed in silence, thinking of when he followed Nur to the rocky outcrop and watched from a distance when the boy gazed into the night sky. Then, as now, Joachim knew this young man had come to them not only as an orphan, but as someone different. Not different as each person differs from others, but unique in a spiritual way he could not comprehend—a child much more than simply an orphan.

Those who watched later spoke of what they had seen. They said it was an unspoken communication—something unique, exceeding the love and nurturing from a parent to a child or from a sibling to a sibling. Jesus came into the world as the Son of God, but the youngster Nur? What had passed between them?

Nur returned from the fields on the afternoon of the twenty-eighth day, carrying flowers and wild herbs he gathered to help overcome the stench of the cave. In the distance, he saw a caravan coming toward them. Its immensity and grandeur overwhelmed him—three distinctive components, each centered on what appeared to be a prestigious person astride a Bactrian two-humped camel. Each man, his camel, and the surrounding dromedaries, asses, men, and women servants constituted a section of the overall caravan which stretched over the lowlands nearly three furlongs.

Nur ran into the cave breathlessly. "Father, Mother," he shouted between gasps of breath. "Come and look."

Joseph bolted from his resting place, not knowing what to expect. He had heard reports of robbers pillaging the poor. Stepping into the sunlight and shielding his eyes with his hand, he looked in the direction Nur pointed, then sighed with relief. The caravan came to pay homage because they had heard the good news. Word of the child had spread throughout the land and beyond its frontier. These people of wealth had traveled a great distance to this hillside overlooking Bethlehem.

They arrived late in the afternoon. Nur ran down the hill to greet them but hesitated when they approached, overcome by the grandeur of what he saw. He froze, unable to move. Heavy blankets draped the backs of camels. Their bodies flowed with each awkward step. Servants scurried ahead to prepare the way for their masters. The sounds of hooves, bells, and trinkets hanging around the necks of the animals filled the air. People spoke to each other in languages unfamiliar to him. They came to bear witness to and adore the child.

After the last animal of the caravan passed, Nur ran back up the hill to help Joseph greet the visitors. Menservants unloaded the camels and donkeys and spread blankets on the ground for their masters to rest while the women prepared tents on the hillside. The well-trained servants quickly moved the animals into other caves and fields to graze.

Three men approached the mouth of the cave. Nur stood aside with Anne and Joachim as Joseph stepped forward to greet them. He bowed his head respectfully, but the first of the men touched his cheek. "No, sir, do not pay homage to us. We come from a great distance and seek only to give." He kissed Joseph on the cheek and stepped aside as the others did the same.

The first man, whose skin manifested the color of desert sand, wore leather sandals, a long purple robe hemmed with silk threads, and a golden-colored mantle around his shoulders. "My name is Theokeno," he said, then stepped aside.

The second man, dressed similarly to the first but with less grandeur to his garments, stepped forward. "And I am Mensor." He bowed at the waist, then moved aside for their companion.

The third man, a man of ebony skin, dressed in an exquisite blue tunic and mantle, approached Joseph and bowed at the waist. Looking into Joseph's eyes, he introduced himself. "I am Sair," he said, then stepped back as Theokeno moved forward.

Theokeno spoke for the three of them. "We witnessed the gathering of stars in the sky as they became one and have followed them to watch their passing." He paused briefly, then put his hands on Joseph's shoulders. "But more so, we come because we believe in what we have witnessed and will witness in the future."

He turned to the others, who in turn looked to their servants. The darkest servant, who was stripped above the waist, moved first. He carried a large trunk to the entrance of the cave. Behind him came a second man, smaller but of sinewy muscles, also stripped above the waist. He held a small golden vase. Then the third servant, a woman of light skin and dark hair which flowed over her shoulders, stepped forward, holding a small wooden trunk.

Joseph spoke. "My wife and child are here. Bring your people to see." He took Nur's hand and led the entourage inside. Theokeno, Mensor, and Sair prostrated themselves before the sleeping baby. His mother sat alongside the crib where animals had once eaten. Her innocent beauty radiated throughout the cave, filling kings and servants with awe as they gazed upon her and the child. Mensor rose and stepped forward, prostrating himself beside the crib at Mary's feet. "We bring gifts to honor this child and your family," he said.

Sair stepped forward next, also prostrating himself beside the crib. "I, too, come to pay homage and give you treasures from my home."

Theokeno, because of his age, fell to his knees and held on to the side of the crib to balance himself. He uttered a slight moan, as his bones and muscles were tired. "And I bring gifts from my home to give to you. Take all I have because you have given more than I possess, and this child will give even more."

A servant helped the older man to his feet, and together the three men stepped back from the crib.

"Your eyes have seen, but before that, your hearts believed," Mary said. "Blessed are you, wise travelers, and blessed are your homes. Speaking for our Son, I thank you and offer His blessing to you."

Another thirteen days passed before Anne and Joachim began their journey back to Nazareth, leaving Nadab and Rachel behind to help Mary and her family. Soon, the time arrived for the purification when they would take the child to the temple in Jerusalem. Nadab and Rachel left a day earlier to arrange for lodging. Joseph and Nur spent the afternoon before their departure preparing packs for the two donkeys and cleaning the cave, which would be memorialized for centuries to come.

A few visitors came late in the afternoon. After seeing the child, Joseph shared with them the gifts the Holy Family had received from more prosperous visitors.

At nightfall, Nur and Joseph prepared a simple meal, then the family ate and went to bed. Mary slept behind a curtain hung from the rafters of the cave and held in place with timbers. She lay close to the crib with her blanket rolled tightly about her. Jesus slept in the manger, wrapped in a warm blanket and shielded from a breeze that swept around the cold walls. Nur and Joseph slept near the entrance where they could guard against trespassers. All slept soundly, tired from the day's activity but ready to begin the short trip to Jerusalem and the longer journey to their home in Nain.

The cock crowed when the paling darkness stole away. The men placed the heaviest load on the back of the lead ass and only a few linens and other small objects on the second animal. Nur laid a blanket across the donkey's back, then went down onto his hands and knees so Mary could climb onto his back and onto the jenny.

Joseph held the baby while she mounted, then Nur jumped to his feet, took the child, and handed Him to Mary.

Thus began the journey of the life of the Messiah.

Chapter Five
The Presentation

Upon reaching Jerusalem in the late afternoon, Joseph and his family found Nadab waiting anxiously at the Sheep Gate. Wearing a freshly washed tunic and sandals, he jumped to his feet and ran down the dusty road to meet them. "Master!" he shouted.

"Hail, Nadab, my friend," Joseph replied. "What good news do you have for us?"

"Lodging, sir." Nadab smiled, satisfied with his success in finding suitable quarters for them. "The city is full of travelers, but Rachel's cousin, Sapphira, found the perfect place for you. It is outside the north wall." He raised his eyebrow and continued. "The owners risked the dangers of the open countryside with its peace and tranquility against the dangers posed by robbers who sometimes roam outside the walls."

A smile creased his lips when he turned and reached a helping hand to Mary while she slipped down from the donkey, holding the child Jesus to her bosom.

Adjusting the veil over her hair and brushing the dust off her clothes, she returned his smile, then kissed his cheek lightly. "Words cannot express my love for you and Rachel," she said. "You have been so helpful during these trying but joyful times." She took a half-step back with tears in her eyes and spoke soft, tender words to him. "Nadab, you may never know in this life the rewards you are earning in the heavenly kingdom, but they are greater in number than the stars in the sky."

Upon hearing her blessed words, Nadab wiped the tears from his eyes with his cuff, bowed his head slightly, and replied, "I know not the truth of your child, but God's angels direct my wife and me to be your companions to the ends of the earth if you so desire." Biting his lip to control his powerful emotions, he turned again to Joseph. "Your family will have a private room and a well with good, sweet water nearby. The house is wonderful, and those living close by are good people—parents, grandparents, and plenty of little ones running about." He shrugged his shoulders and smiled. "It is a proper respite from your travels."

"My special friend," Mary said as she rocked the child to and fro to calm His squirming little body, "only God in heaven can repay you for all you have done for us."

Joseph, too, spoke. "Nadab, to sleep in a house is far greater than anything else you could do for us. It has been a long while. Too long!" He squeezed Nadab's hands, then put his arms around him and hugged his friend wholeheartedly.

With Nur at his side, Nadab led them beyond the Sheep Gate and turned north. Pointing to a steep hill outside the wall, Nur asked in his innocent, childish voice, "What is that place?"

"That? It's something we don't talk about," Nadab replied hurriedly. "Let me tell you about where you will sleep tonight. It is—"

"No," Nur said, his voice now strong and determined. He pointed back to the hill. "Tell me about that. I want to know."

Nadab looked back over his shoulder. He and Nur were some distance ahead of the family. He frowned and shook his head. Sometimes Nur could irritate him, and his pushy questions sometimes illustrated his youthful annoyance. "Well, my curious little one, if you must know, I will tell you, but you should not talk to your mother about it. Do you understand?"

Nur nodded.

"That is Golgotha."

"What?"

"Golgotha," Nadab barked. "Golgotha, where they execute people. Now that you know, you can forget it." He quickened his pace and moved ahead of the boy.

"Forget? No, my good friend," Nur said, looking back at the hill again. "No, I will never forget."

Rachel roused them early, long before the sun brightened the day for the presentation of Jesus in the temple. Nur watched in silence while everyone prepared for the day. Mary wore the same blue garment she wore for the circumcision, while Joseph wore a dark brown robe that hung to the tops of his sandaled feet. Over that, he wore a bleached white Greek tunic, a *chiton*. A wide leather belt on his waist held a purse containing the coins for presentation to the priests. He looked elegant, not like a carpenter, but the most respected merchant in the land.

Rachel told Nur that today would be a special day with the presentation of many baby boys. The rabbi had written Jesus' name at the top of the scroll to be first, so they had to eat quickly and be on their way. Nur dressed hurriedly, grabbing a small loaf of bread as they entered the courtyard.

"May I light the way, Father?" he asked when he reached for a torch at the gateway.

"Indeed, you may," Joseph responded. He and Nadab helped Mary onto the back of the donkey. She scooted around on the blanket with her legs dangling to the side, then took the child from Rachel, and they left the compound for the walled city.

Nur led them into the street, carrying the torch and lighting the way for the presentation of the Messiah in the temple. The pathway led to the west wall of the city, but rather than going through the Galilee gate, they followed the road they'd traveled yesterday, passing Golgotha and then through the gate and into the city. Jerusalem still slept. In the early morning silence, the clomping of the donkeys' hooves echoed off the narrow, cobbled streets, reverberating against the houses and shops that crowded against each other. Somewhere a dog barked, and elsewhere a baby cried.

Nadab directed Nur through twists and turns in the narrow streets. They passed through a gate in another wall before coming onto a wide roadway leading to the high wall surrounding the temple. Nur slowed his pace, looking over his shoulder to make sure the others were close behind him even though he could hear their footsteps clearly in the morning quiet. The size of the wall surrounding the temple intimidated him with its overwhelming magnitude. When he approached the gate, an old man came from the direction of the temple.

A cold chill ran up Nur's spine as the old man scooted his feet along, coughing and wheezing, but extending his arm and hand toward the baby.

"Hail, my friends," the old man said in a loud whisper. "I am Simeon, and I have awaited your arrival." He bowed low from the waist, then approached Joseph, Mary, and the child.

Joseph stopped the donkey and greeted the man with a slight nod. "You say you are Simeon. Do we know you?"

"No, kind sir, you do not." Simeon shook his grizzled head. "The angel of God foretold your arrival, and I have come to greet you."

Nur watched as Nadab moved toward the stranger.

"What do you say, old man?" Nadab commanded.

Before Simeon could reply, Joseph raised his hand to stop Nadab from further inquiry.

"The Lord God has indeed sent a messenger to you, Simeon," Joseph replied. "You are a righteous man and shall share the Kingdom of Heaven with all of the angels of the Lord."

Simeon looked at Mary and Jesus. "Blessed among all women are you, the mother of the Savior." Tears welled in his eyes as he stepped forward, gently moving the veil covering the child's face. "And, most holy are you, child, Son of the Living God." Simeon stepped back. Tears poured from his eyes. "May the Lord God lift my soul from these lands. I have believed and witnessed all the words spoken by the prophets. The glory of the Most High is upon you."

He turned, shuffling his feet as he headed back to the temple. He took only a few steps when he stopped. Turning toward Mary, he started to speak, then paused as though he did not know how to proceed. A touch of a smile crossed his lips, and with a polite nod in recognition of her, he spoke. "Behold, this child is set for the fall and rising of many in Israel and for a sign which shall be spoken against. Yea, a sword shall pierce thy own heart, my good lady."

Nur watched guardedly as Rachel and Nadab embraced in fear but prepared to bear witness to the truth. Joseph also stood frozen, one arm resting across the child who slept in His mother's arms.

After Simeon faded into the darkness, Joseph and the others looked at each other. "Lead on," Joseph said to Nur. "Into the temple."

They passed through the outer wall of the grand temple into the spacious courtyard. Nur absorbed the sights that greeted his curious eyes: fountains and flowers, men and women resting on benches surrounding small altars, roses, and other sweet buds bordering stone walkways. Tranquility embraced them. This place contrasted sharply with the close and crowded city streets. Nur allowed Joseph to take the lead, falling behind the donkey to grasp the grandeur of this magnificent, holy place.

An old woman approached them, introducing herself as Anna. She spoke briefly to Joseph, who introduced her to his wife and child. From the donkey's back, Joseph removed the large basket of fresh fruit he had brought as a gift. He gave it to Anna to present to the priests. Then he took a cage containing two turtledoves and gave them to a second woman.

Mary handed the child to her husband and, holding Nur's hand for support, slipped down from the donkey. Taking Jesus back from Joseph, they followed the women into the temple.

Nur walked behind them, mesmerized by the immensity and grandeur of the temple.

Entering the massive double doors, he saw three altars in the center of the room, one much larger than the others. Fine white linens draped the large center altar. Linens of various shades of red, trimmed in gold and silver, covered the linen. A large silver chalice rested in the center of the altar. The two side altars appeared bare and foreboding without any adornments. One held a large wicker basket, the other a wooden dish. Burning candles and silver flasks of oil flanked each altar on three sides.

Men and women sat at the back of the main room to attend the rites of the first-born Son's presentation in the temple and Mary's purification in obedience to the Torah.

Anna carried the fruit and placed it in the wooden dish. The second woman placed the cage of doves in the wicker basket on the other altar.

Joseph and the family waited at the door until three priests entered from a side door. The priests, wearing the finest vestments of the temple, walked to the center altar and opened a large scroll that one of them carried over his head. They prayed in unison, chanted softly, then turned to Joseph and his family, motioning them forward.

Nur stayed near the door.

Mary clasped the child tightly to her bosom as they approached the priests. They were a few steps away when Joseph took Jesus and gave Him to the priest in the middle, who immediately raised the baby in the air over his head.

As the priest's hands touched the child, the scent of roses overwhelmed the aroma of the incense. An iridescent glow descended from the ceiling, brighter over the center altar but softer over the others. The colors of the rainbow bathed everyone present, bringing an aura of peace to the holy ceremony.

Nur looked toward the high ceiling and saw the temple filled with the joyful faces of the cherubim and seraphim singing hymns to the honor and glory of the Almighty.

Mary and Joseph saw the marvelous sight. But for Anna, the others sat attentive and stone-faced, unaware of the heavenly chorus about them. The rainbow of soft colors took on an indescribable brightness, and Nur bowed his head to shield his eyes.

Mary and Joseph also bowed their heads. The power and glory of God descended upon them with the majesty of the Most High. While angels' songs joined together to God's delight, the dedication of the first-born male child brought fulfillment to the Law and the Prophets.

Nur watched quietly and understood. The Son of God, the Messiah, Jesus the Christ, had come as an innocent child to accept His role in delivering the souls of Jews and gentiles into the Kingdom of Heaven.

Each priest held the child overhead, turning in the four directions and calling out His name. "Jesus," they shouted. "The son of Joseph is dedicated to our Lord God." Twelve times they called his name, then returned the baby to His mother.

Joseph stepped to the altar, loosened his purse, and placed the thirty coins of silver into the chalice on the altar. Upon completion of the ceremony, the family stepped back from the altar and walked solemnly toward the doors.

Anna hurried after them. "Stop, please! Allow me to touch this child who has come among us."

Mary removed the veil covering Jesus' face and turned Him toward her.

"I did not see what you saw or that which overcame you," the old woman exclaimed, "but in my heart, I know this is the child the prophets spoke of in the years of our ancestors!" She smiled and looked at the baby, now fast asleep in His mother's arms. Anna reached out a gnarled, arthritic finger and touched the child's cheek. "I am blessed," she said as she looked at Mary. "Blessed are you, the mother of the Savior. And you too, sir," she said to Joseph. "My life is fulfilled because of this child Jesus, and may His bold light always shine upon you."

"May the Lord's blessing always be with you," replied Mary.

The family returned to their lodgings, walking carefully through the now crowded streets, dodging children playing and men delivering their goods to the marketplace. It had become a vibrant, exciting place—crowded walkways, merchants presenting their wares for sale, women shopping, animals en route to market, and the general hubbub and noise of city life.

Nur took a deep breath and relaxed when they passed through the gate into the openness of the outer city. The clean, cool air refreshed him as they followed the road that traversed Golgotha, where Jesus became restless and began to cry.

Nur, too, felt restless and turned to look at the site of men's execution. He understood, and his heart filled with sorrow. He moved closer to Mary, who held the child on her lap as she rode upon the donkey.

"Give me His hand," Nur said.

Mary pulled Jesus' hand from beneath the blanket, and Nur took it. At the touching of their hands, the child quieted. "You have a special talent," Mary said with a sweet smile creasing her lips.

The boy smiled, happy that he'd quieted the baby, then glanced at Mary. "Thank you, Mother," he whispered.

They spent the rest of the day preparing to leave the city for the journey to Galilee. Nur longed to return there with his new parents and his baby brother, the Son of God. A newfound life awaited each of them—a life of love and sorrow, peace and pain, and a plethora of great expectations and surprises. Nur's heart brimmed with excitement because he understood that which many would never understand.

The Messiah lived among them!

Chapter Six
Flight to Egypt

The fading rays of the golden sun flickered over the distant hilltops. Everyone had eaten their fill. They were exhausted from the day's activity and needed rest for the long trip home to Nain. Nur, Rachel, and Nadab put the house in order while the others prepared for bed.

The moon rode high in the sky, its blue hue slipping through the window screens. Before retiring, Joseph took one last peek behind the screen providing privacy for Mary and Jesus. Sleeping on her back and bathed in the moonlight, she held the Christ Child in the crook of her arms.

Joseph smiled inwardly, his heart and soul at peace. Tiptoeing through the house, he found Nur asleep on a pad alongside Joseph's mat. Another screen separated them from Rachel and Nadab opposite their sleeping area.

While in a deep sleep, Nur felt a gentle tap on his shoulder. Opening his eyes, he saw Joseph sound asleep but turning over. Assuming Joseph had bumped him, Nur adjusted his pad and returned to sleep. Moments later, it happened again—someone tapped his shoulder. With his eyes still closed, he scooted a few inches farther from Joseph, only to be roused a third time. Opening his eyes wide, he lay on his back and stretched. Joseph remained asleep.

A voice in the darkness whispered in his ear, "Nur, arise and warn the others. The Son of God is in danger."

Sitting up straight, Nur saw the faintest shadow of a person standing between Joseph and him.

The image leaned forward, close to his ear. "Arise and go. All of you must flee immediately. Herod's soldiers are under orders to slay every male baby." The image's hand rested on Nur's shoulder. "Wake the others. The soldiers arrive before the cock crows." Stepping back, the image whispered another command. "Take the child to Egypt. Herod fears the newborn King of the Jews and is slaughtering the innocents. Return when you receive assurance that no harm will befall the Messiah."

Nur bolted to his feet and gasped for breath. His heart pounded. Gripped with fear, he hesitated only a moment but understood what he must do. "Father," he whispered into Joseph's ear while he shook his shoulders.

Joseph barely opened his eyes. "Go back to sleep, boy. Be quiet, or you'll wake the others."

"No, Father. We must flee! We must go now." He leaned forward, close to Joseph's face. "The soldiers will slay Him if we don't go this moment."

Joseph jumped to his feet, nearly knocking over the screen that separated them from Nadab and his wife. "What is this you say, child?" he demanded in a whispered voice.

Nur stood before Joseph, the moon's rays washing over his little body. "I tell you the truth, Father. We must take Him and go. We have to run, but we cannot go home. Only in Egypt will He be safe."

"What are you telling me?" Joseph demanded.

From the other side of the screen, Nadab heard their voices and rose. "What is it?"

Nur's voice quaked as he spoke. "Herod has commanded the death of all baby boys. We must flee now. There is no time to waste." Tears flowed down his cheeks. He gasped for his breath. "Herod fears the child who will be the King of the Jews. His army will pull many babies from their mothers' arms and slaughter them." He pointed to where Jesus and Mary slept and began to cry aloud. "They will kill Him if we do not flee."

Joseph and Nadab looked at each other. They were bewildered. How could this youngster know what they should do?

"Tell us all you know," Joseph demanded.

"That *is* what I know, Father!" he cried. "They are killing all the baby boys because they fear the King of the Jews. We cannot remain here. We must take him to Egypt! We will suffer many hardships but can return to Galilee when it is safe." Exhausted, he let out a deep breath and dropped to the floor. "That is all I know."

"Surely this boy has received a message from God," Joseph said. "We must go."

As he spoke, Rachel rose from her mat and dressed for the journey.

Joseph tapped softly on the doorframe, slid the screen aside, and entered. Mary lay on her stomach, only the top of her head protruding from beneath the cover. She had the Christ Child wrapped in a small blanket and tucked in alongside her. Joseph knelt beside her, touched her shoulder, and spoke softly into her ear. "Mary, Mary. We need to leave."

Mary rolled onto her side and opened her eyes. "Joseph, what are you doing? It's the middle of the night. Did you have a bad dream?"

He lifted her to a sitting position and held her tightly. "No. Not a dream. A messenger of God has spoken to Nur." Every gesture and movement Joseph made reflected the misfortune they faced—his voice somber, shoulders slumped, and his voice quaking. "We must flee now, or they will kill Jesus."

"No!" Mary whispered fiercely. "They cannot harm Him. We must go."

Once again, the family followed the donkey that led them from Nain to Bethlehem, but their new destination lay far across the scorching desert—Egypt. The moonlight painted the quiet countryside with a heavenly glow. An occasional dog bark broke the silence. They traveled a path unknown to them but would lead them to their new home, wherein they would be foreigners. The donkey took them near Golgotha and to the Bethlehem road, then turned abruptly to the west onto a seldom-used trail that led into the rugged countryside.

Nur walked beside the donkey carrying Mary and Jesus, with a few bundles tied to its rump. Nadab followed but carried a large pack over his shoulder. They had traveled only a short distance, the walls of Jerusalem still in sight under the moonlit sky, when the baby stirred. The others moved ahead and provided privacy for Mary to feed Him.

They held the Kingdom of God in their hands and would not stop until they knew the baby Jesus no longer faced Herod's wrath.

By the time the sun rose over the mountaintops, they had approached the village of Ain Karim. Mary's kinswoman, Elizabeth, lived there with her husband, Zacharias, and their son, John. The donkey led them directly to the door of the house. While Joseph told Elizabeth and Zacharias the reason for their journey, Mary changed the baby's clothes. Nur fed and watered the animals, and then the travelers continued west, now accompanied by Elizabeth and her young son, John.

They continued along the trail through rugged hills and barren wasteland of sandstone and limestone. Out of sight of their home, Elizabeth directed them to stop. Holding her child in her arms, Mary slid down from the donkey and took her cousin in her arms. They embraced each other and each other's child.

With his teetering little gait, Elizabeth took John's hand and led him toward a steep hill dotted with old caves. Less than a year old, John could not walk on the trail, so Elizabeth hoisted him onto her back, carrying him and their pack of clothing and food.

Zacharias would watch for strangers or soldiers, and only when he felt confident that they were free from danger would he deliver provisions to them. They would stay in the caves until the threat to boys under the age of two had passed.

The lead ass started its slow, plodding pace through the hills again. Nur walked beside it, and Mary sat on its back. Nur carried a skin of water over his shoulder. He drank it dry by mid-afternoon, but the others had barely touched theirs.

"Child, drink with caution because we do not know where we will next find fresh water," Joseph advised him.

"I'm sorry, Father. I'll not drink again without your approval." He put his hand beneath the blanket and took hold of His tiny foot. Looking up at Mary, he said, "I'll stay with Him and help you if you need me." He looked over his shoulder at Joseph and smiled, then their caravan crossed a dry creek bed and started up another rocky, barren hill.

The grueling hours slipped away. The shadows grew long, and the heat of the afternoon sun began to fade. They went down a steep track into a craggy and desolate ravine. Joseph looked at Mary and saw how pale her cheeks had become. At the same time, Jesus began to squirm and cry. Joseph knew they could go no farther.

"Here," he said. He didn't know where they were but assumed they had traveled far enough to be reasonably safe. Nevertheless, in the wilderness, they would have to watch for snakes, scorpions, and wild dogs that lived in the hills. He knew Nur, Nadab, and he would get little sleep.

Mary slid off the little jenny. Holding the child tightly in her arms and speaking softly to conserve her energy, she said directly to Joseph, "Yes, I am tired and need rest, but we must keep our spirits lifted to God Almighty. He will test our faith, and we will demonstrate we can accomplish His commands."

Carefully holding her child, she leaned forward and kissed her husband on the cheek.

A solitary tear formed in Joseph's eye. He wiped it with his cuff, smiled, and spread a blanket on the ground where she could lean against a boulder. "Give me your hand," he said as he assisted her in sitting back in reasonable comfort, now holding the child to her breast.

The men and Nur removed the packs from the animals and made a camp. Nadab felt the waterskins and found them scorched by the desert sun. He opened one, tasted the water, and found it tepid.

Mary covered herself and the child to feed Him, but still, He began to cry. "Oh, Joseph, what have I done that this child deserves this? Why should He suffer in His innocence?" Mary looked at Jesus with pleading and tearful eyes.

Joseph, his lips parched, spoke softly. "Nothing, my blessed wife. You have done nothing, nor has any of us sinned and brought this against us."

He sat beside her and leaned back against the rock. "We do not need to understand why. We both want to know, but it is our responsibility to do as God commands. He instructs that you and I, with the help of our friends, take this child to the ends of the earth if need be."

While Rachel prepared the meager food for their meal, Nur explored, climbing over rocks and walking down the ravine. He had been gone a few minutes when Joseph heard him cry out, not in a frightened voice, but joyfully. Nur ran back over the rocks toward them, smiling and laughing.

"Look what I found!" he yelled. They all began to laugh as they saw his find—mud. Soggy, dripping mud. Nur had found water.

Nadab and Joseph laughed as he threw mud at each of them, missing both times. They followed him back down the gully and found a slow trickling spring between two layers of rock. The water flowed into the sandy bottom, which quickly absorbed it.

Joseph spoke to Nur. "Run. Get the skins."

Without waiting for directions, Nadab scooped out the sand with his bare hands to make a dish-sized pit to trap the water.

Minutes later, Nur returned with the five waterskins, pausing to dump the tepid one into the dry sand.

Together, the men sat on the edge of the ravine while Nur lowered the skins into the pit. Upon filling the first container, he jumped to his feet and scurried back to Mary so she could taste her reward for their harrowing day.

The water flowed slowly as the fading rays of the desert sun beat down upon them. The setting sun threw its luminous rays across the desert floor before they completed filled the skins. Nevertheless, all of them were happy.

Nadab and Joseph took turns on the lookout for the remainder of the night while the others slept, wrapped snugly in their blankets.

For the next two days, the little caravan moved southwest across the bleak, featureless country—hills and ravines, rocks and more rocks, and a scorching sun. The donkey led them in what sometimes seemed like aimless meandering, but each day they found fresh, clear water. Nevertheless, the relentless desert heat weighed on them. The wind burned their faces, dried their eyes, and sapped their strength. The challenge had become unending.

At times, Mary worried the steady jarring of the animal's hoofs on the hard ground would make her child sick. Still, whenever she felt despair, they found a shady spot to rest or a spring to fill their water bags and wash the grit from their faces. Their food, though tasteless, was substantial and would hold them for several more days.

The third day brought them to the outskirts of Eglon. Joseph had visited there before on business and found it to be a place that did not welcome visitors. He ordered Nur to stop the donkeys on a bluff overlooking the city, fearful of placing Jesus and the rest of them in harm's way.

Mary looked Joseph in the eye, bit her lip, and expressed herself in a stern voice she seldom used. "Joseph, we must go in," she commanded. "Our food is nearly gone, our animals are exhausted, our child needs to rest, and look at us." She gestured in a sweeping motion at each of them. "We're tired and hungry and dirty and thirsty." She paused for a moment, then got off her donkey. "Joseph," she said as tears streaked the dirt on her face. "We're tired...so tired."

"I agree, Master," said Nadab. "We must take the risk." He pointed to the vast Negev desert in the distance. "That lies between us and Egypt. Surely, sir, the Lord God has heard our prayers and allowed us to find this place."

Joseph looked at Nur. "You, my son, have been filled with so much wisdom throughout this—" He paused. "—this command of God. What do you say?"

"I will follow wherever you go," the youngster replied. "Wherever you are, there I will be."

Joseph stood with his fists folded tightly on his hips. He looked at the hard ground beneath his feet, shook his head, then looked at the others. "Let us go into the city." His strong voice reflected his concern but acknowledged the necessity of moving forward. Looking down into Eglon, he took a deep breath and smiled through his parched lips. "The Lord God will guide and care for us." He put his hand on his wife's shoulder and looked at his sleeping Son. "Eglon is where we'll rest before the desert. Come."

Nur led the way into the city, where they promptly learned their fears were unwarranted. Merchants and innkeepers welcomed their business, and the people graciously opened their hearts to these travelers who looked so tired and miserable. The entourage found lodgings with sufficient space for each to have some privacy and fresh water so they could drink their fill, clean the filth from their bodies, and wash their clothes.

Refreshed by nightfall, they enjoyed a meal with the innkeeper, his wife, and his children. Joseph's previous experience from earlier trips was now a thing of the past, for the people were kind and generous. God had indeed answered their prayers.

They rested there for the next day and night, then began their journey into the bleak and foreboding desert, away from their homeland. They stayed off the main highways for fear of soldiers or robbers but followed the donkey's slow, plodding pace over faint trails, into the ravines and dry riverbeds, up steep barren hills, yet always away from home and on toward Egypt.

The days offered a blinding sun and scorching wind that picked up grains of sand that pelted their skin and burned their eyes; nights brought hard ground, often with only a few remaining drops of water and a cold breeze to pierce their garments.

"Surely," Joseph said one morning, "our Lord God is putting us to the test. I have no idea why this is happening but have faith that we must continue for His sake."

Mary wet her parched lips, kissed his cheek, and replied, "So be it. We will do as commanded by God." She smiled and began to sing the song of Moses and Mariam, which she recalled from her childhood. Rachel joined in, and they continued their trek to Egypt in the name of the Father and of the Son.

Chapter Seven
Robbers

On their seventh day in the wilderness, they reached a bluff with a commanding view of the rugged mountains and scorching desert standing between them and Egypt. Leaning into the wind and shielding his eyes from the sun, Nur squinted at the distant hills. His eyes did not deceive him—several dilapidated mud buildings clung to a steep-walled canyon in their intended path. He stopped, and the others halted behind him. "Father, come look," he called while pointing to the scene ahead.

Joseph hastened forth and climbed a boulder for a better view. Surely whoever lived in such quarters could not portend well for them. He knew the stories about the ravages vile men heaped upon weary travelers. The evildoers often lived in desolate places where small caravans had to pass.

Joseph murmured softly, more to himself than to the others, "My God in heaven, what bodes for us in this unforgiving land?" Sweat dotted his forehead as he turned to Nadab, who had followed him to their vantage point. Joseph grimaced, shaking his head in doubt as he spoke. "What are your thoughts?"

"We have little choice but to continue," Nadab replied. "It's a full day's journey to go back and find another way around." He pointed in the direction from which they had come. "We don't have enough food or water to do anything but go forward."

Nur, who had climbed up with them, agreed with a simple nod. "Father, this donkey led us here, and we must have faith in God. However evil these men may be, no harm will come to us. I'm confident of it."

Scooting down from the rock, they gathered together for a brief prayer, then moved forward with faith that the Lord God would protect them.

They were duty-bound to believe in Him, to have faith, and all else would come to pass.

When they approached the entrance to the canyon, Nur heard a voice call out to them sarcastically, "Welcome." He looked up and saw an old man, dirty and tattered, standing amidst a scattering of acacia trees and rocks. The man laughed at them. "What kind of people are you? You bring us no riches, but we will take what we want before we permit people to pass." He smirked. "*If* we allow you the privilege."

The man climbed down from his perch, brushed past Nur, and spoke to Joseph, "You, my friend, must be poorer than we, the outcasts of the world." He stretched out his arm and gestured to their miserable homes. "We live in exile but have greater wealth than you."

Standing beside his wife and child, Joseph looked with complete confidence into the man's eyes. "We come in the name of God. We are going to Egypt and seek only to rest for a short time and to drink of your water." He bowed his head respectfully to the old man and continued. "With your blessings, we will do so and then be on our way."

Several other filthy men and women and a few children dressed in rags gathered to block the narrow trail. The dirty old man, apparently the leader, stepped past Joseph and reached out to Mary. He gently removed the blanket under which Jesus rested in His mother's lap.

"What have we here?" he questioned as he stepped back and frowned, glancing back and forth between Mary and Joseph. "A baby? What kind of parents are you that you travel in such conditions with a baby? This is but a newborn and shouldn't travel in this land."

With her soft but emphatic voice, Mary pleaded, "Sir, the soldiers are killing all babies, and we are fleeing for our child's life. We humbly seek your kindness, for we must move on until this innocent babe is safe from the Romans. Will you help us?"

At that moment, the baby wiggled His tiny body and reached out and grasped the man's finger.

"Well, look at this," he shouted to his friends. "He likes me! Yes, my friends, you are safe with us. Come." He put his arm around Joseph's shoulders. "Come and share what little we have, for the gods look with favor on us that you should visit."

"No," Joseph barked as he shoved the man's hand from his shoulder. "Not the gods! The one God Most High who will bring salvation to you and your children and their children."

"Whatever you say," the man replied with a shrug and gesture. "Anyway, you are welcome here."

He led them to a crumbling structure tucked in the shade of the canyon walls. His wife stood at the doorway of their home, a few grimy rags draped around her body, her toothless mouth grinning at the visitors.

"You people look as lost as anyone I have ever seen," she said. "What brings you our way?" She didn't give them a chance to respond before she continued. "We don't get many people here, and what few we get usually leave their riches with us." She threw her head back and opened her mouth wide as she cackled at her own humor. "Anyway, my husband is our leader." She shrugged. "If he says you're welcome, then so be it."

She helped Mary and the child off the donkey while Nur and the men unloaded their packs.

"Come in," the old woman said. "Don't be afraid. We won't hurt you." She nodded toward a shelf hanging precariously on the wall. "Look, I have fresh bread." She turned and pointed toward a mat on the dirt floor. "Here, sit and rest while I get you some water and food."

Mary tucked Jesus under her garments and fed Him while the woman fetched the bread.

She cracked a hint of a smile when she turned back to Mary. "Well, you still have your milk, so you must be doing better than you look. But you need to eat, too." She ripped off a chunk of bread and passed it to Mary.

Mary spoke softly. "Thank you for your generosity, my lady."

"My lady? Ho!" the hag cackled. "It's been so long since anyone called me a lady that I am unable remember." Using her dirty, crusty, and arthritic bare foot, she scooted a mat close to Mary and sat beside her. "Everyone considered me to be a lady in high standing, but many years have passed, so many years," she uttered as her voice trailed off.

"Tell me," Mary asked, "how did you come to live here, so far from everywhere? So alone?"

The old lady hung her head, rubbed her hands together, and looked into Mary's eyes. With her head bowed in humiliation but her eyes upcast to Mary, she spoke. "My husband held a position of high esteem. A merchant, and an honest one, too—things he made or imported from Asia. We lived in Jerusalem and Bethlehem. He sold only the finest linens and the most valuable silver and gold jewelry for ladies." She looked back into her lap, grimaced her lips, and nodded.

"We had a married daughter. Her husband, Seth, worked with my husband, but he did not have an honest trait in his body." Tears welled in the old woman's eyes." He stole from our customers and from us, too. He pocketed money from a wealthy man—Laban, a thriving linen and jewelry dealer. Seth thought his thievery would not be detected, but Laban's clerk caught onto him. Laban went into in a rage."

Shaking her head as tears streaked through the grime of her dirty face, she caught her breath and continued. "Laban held power and influence in the area. He gave the order for his servants to take our daughter's husband into the field and stone him. Seth prided himself on thievery but did not deserve what happened to him. Laban made us watch, and as much as we detested what Seth had done, we begged for his mercy." She nodded her head slowly. "Our pleas fell on deaf ears." She paused, breathed deeply, and allowed the tears to flow from her eyes. "Seth died a terrible death and left us with a pregnant daughter."

The old woman paused and stared at the floor of her wretched home. She dabbed her eyes with her cuff and continued. "Then Edna, our only daughter, died giving birth to our grandson. We lost everything, and in shame, we fled. Now look at us." She spread her hands and looked about. "This is all we have, so we steal what we need."

Compassion for the old lady filled Mary's heart.

Before she could continue, a small boy, no older than three or four years old, ran into the house. "Grandmother," he bellowed, "why didn't we take these peoples' clothes and send them on their way?" Suddenly, he saw Mary and the baby sitting in the corner. "Oh, I didn't know they were in here," he said sheepishly as he began to back up.

"Hush!" the old woman snapped. "Show these people that we have manners." She reached for a clay pot on the shelf and handed it to him. "Take this and fill it with water so this lady can wash her child. Come over here and look at him, just a little thing."

The boy stepped warily across the room and knelt beside Mary, who raised her child so the boy could see Him.

"His name is Jesus. What is yours?"

"Elam," the boy replied, then ran out the doorway to fetch the water. Shortly, he returned with the bowl full to the brim. "Here! Wash your baby. Can I watch?"

"Yes, you can," Mary replied while she dabbed a cloth in the water and began to wash the Son of God. When the wet cloth touched His face, Jesus opened His sleepy eyes and looked beyond His mother to Elam.

The boy giggled. "Look, Grandmother Marisa, he sees me."

The little boy remained at Mary's side as she bathed Jesus. After washing her Son, she used her veil to dry Him. Then, she washed Elam's hands, face, and feet using the cloth with which she had cleansed Jesus.

Marisa sat quietly and understood the unspoken message from Jesus' mother. It came from Scripture, *netilat yadayim,* a ritual cleansing of sin.

"Elam," said Mary, "the Word of the Lord has come upon you, and you shall reside in paradise."

"You are a holy woman," Marisa said. "Surely the one true God lives in your heart. We are not worthy that you should enter under our roof. This child Jesus, is He the Messiah the prophets spoke of so long ago?"

"Cast aside all false gods, my lady," Mary said, "for you have received the Word of the Lord." As she spoke, the scent of fresh flowers filled the room, and a sense of heavenly peace descended upon them.

After caring for the animals, Nur and the men entered to find Mary and Jesus, Elam, and his grandmother filled with the grace of God. Each of them sat with graceful elegance in their humble surroundings as the glow of a rainbow filled the room. The men stood in respectful silence for a few moments before the old man spoke. "What is this that happens?"

When Marisa told him of the *netilat yadayim*, the cleansing by the one true God, the group's leader fell to his knees, bowed his head, and wept.

"Where has this God been? After what we have been through, I decided the one God did not exist, and that left us these idols we worship." He looked at his visitors; his voice cracked. "We gave up. We were lost. We tried everything, but nothing worked. But now you have come. I do not know why."

He rose to his feet and stepped toward Mary and the child. "I, too, feel His presence in my house. I thank you for coming to us, and I know what we must do." He looked at Marisa and Elam. "We will leave this place and go to Jerusalem. I will ask forgiveness from those I owe, and I will be their slave if need be." He bent over Mary. "My lady, if I may touch this child, I, too, will find salvation."

Upon hearing his words, Mary took his hand and held it to Jesus' forehead, and the gift of the Holy Spirit filled his heart. He looked at his wife. Dazzling white robes replaced her tattered garments. She wore soft slippers on her feet, and her smile radiated as beautifully as when they met many years ago. A tan tunic and sandals replaced Elam's rags. He was clean. Marisa's husband appeared as strong and handsome as a gentleman should look, and his clothes were clean and new.

"Ezor," she said to her husband, "we have received the truth of the Most High, and tomorrow we will go home." She put her hands out to her husband of many years. "I love you, Ezor."

Nur stood silently in the doorway, observing all and knowing the truth of God Almighty, the one who forgives sins and shares His blessings with all who accept His word.

Chapter Eight
Egypt

Resuming their flight to Egypt, they traveled west for seven more days. Following the trials and tribulations of their trek, the eighth day brought them unlimited joy—the Great River. A natural wonder, the river symbolized historic economic, political, and religious importance. It stood as the final obstacle between them and Egypt.

Filled with joy and looking across the broad expanse of the waters, Nadab folded his arms across his chest and spoke confidently. "Our timing is perfect. The river is at its low point of the year, so we should easily find an oarsman to take us to the other side."

Joseph nodded his approval and gathered them all together. "Let us give thanks," he said.

With Nur taking the child in his arms, Mary slid down from the back of the little jenny and went to her knees. Nur handed Jesus to her, and she held Him while the others gathered around, knelt, and joined hands.

As head of the family, Joseph led them in prayer. "We give thanks to You, Almighty God. You have strengthened us to bring this child to Egypt, escape Herod's wrath, and find ourselves tired in body but strong in the faith of Your eternal love. You have blessed us, and we will serve You each day throughout our lives."

Taking a deep breath as he stood, he massaged his aching back, then assisted his wife to her feet, still clutching the child to her bosom.

As the others rose, Nadab turned to Nur. "We have arrived," he said. He put his hand on the youngster's shoulder and gave him a smile and friendly jostle. "You are an excellent guide, my little friend."

"Indeed," Joseph said. "We have fulfilled the command of the One Most High. Now, we must be patient. We know not the time when we can return home. Until then, we will live and work as foreigners in a strange land. Life may not be easy, but we will prevail with guidance from our heavenly Father."

They rested for two days, regaining strength, enjoying the cool waters and the plentiful fruit and shade of the trees. On their third day, they traveled a short distance north and found a river crossing staffed by strong, young men who ferried them across the waterway for a fair price.

Arriving on the western shore, they held hands together and bowed their heads. Joseph again led them in prayer, offering thanks to the Almighty for safeguarding them from the combined Roman and Greek soldiers who carried out the slaughter of the innocents.

Joseph guided them a short distance to a swale beneath a grove of eucalyptus trees where he pitched their camp. With the advantages of being in a hollow, depressed area and the enormous girth of the mature trees, they had shelter from the wind and sun. It would suffice until such time as he could prepare more suitable housing for them.

The men set up a tent for Rachel and Nadab and another for Mary and the baby. Joseph and Nur pitched their mats beneath the trees with their fleece blankets to protect them from dampness from the river.

After a cursory inspection of the expanse of land adjacent to the riverbank, Joseph determined that most of the area's Egyptians lived in small compounds scattered along the shoreline. They earned a modest living from fishing and harvesting fruit from the otherwise lush, well-maintained plantations of fig, olive, apple, and pomegranate trees owned by a few wealthy landowners.

The following day, Nur and the men set out to find permanent housing and a place where they might work in carpentry or masonry. They strode throughout the area, finding little more than crumbling buildings, including the ones in which people lived. The population seemed indifferent to providing decent housing for themselves or their families. They lived slovenly, seemingly without concern for anything more than earning just enough to buy food but little else.

By day's end, they returned, disappointed, having found scant materials to build a new home for themselves. Pulling up a cushion beneath a tree and wiping his brow, Joseph spoke to Mary and Rachel. "Not far from here, we found the remains of an abandoned house. We can manage where we are, but," he reached for Nur and pulled him close, "the three of us will clear the clutter from that crumbling, old place. I think we can make it suitable to live in." He offered a halfhearted chuckle. "It will do. Eventually, we will upgrade it to be a place worthy to call home."

⁂

While Rachel and Nadab faithfully served Joseph and Mary, Jesus' parents never discussed His divinity with them. Nonetheless, they understood they would live in this foreign land until the Lord's messenger assured them of a safe return to their homeland.

Nur proved himself to be a valuable helper to Joseph and Nadab. With his youthful energy and assistance, the house underwent a transition to a livable home in only a few days.

Jesus, the Son of God, would live as an alien—an outcast from His native country. It would be in Egypt that Jesus began His journey of maturation. He took His first step, a toddling three paces before falling on His behind; spoke His first word, father (in Aramaic); tasted His first piece of fruit, a bite of apricot offered by His mother; and played His first game, a foot race with a young Egyptian of Jesus' age.

Nur became His companion and mentor, teaching Him about the birds and insects, the flowers and plants, the fish and the animals. The boys were inseparable as the bond grew between them. Jesus often accompanied Nur to the river, where he would fill their jugs with water for the women who tended the house or the men who worked under the blazing sun for the wealthy landowners.

Time passed slowly. Nur overheard the adults speak about how the Egyptians did not accept them and how harsh they were to their hired foreigners. It had become common for the landowners who hired them not to pay them a fair day's wage for their efforts. Nevertheless, despite the hardships, the family prospered from their hard work. Joseph built tables, beds, and screens from driftwood and the reeds at the river's edge for their own house. They divided the house into rooms so Nadab and Rachel could have a private area and Mary and the child another. Joseph built a small stone building adjacent to the house as sleeping quarters for himself and Nur.

Though their home in Galilee had been better, they accepted their responsibilities in service to Almighty God and adjusted their living standards. They were committed to His will, and they would live here forever if necessary.

Jesus, Mary, Joseph, Nur, Nadab, and Rachel remained in Egypt until long after Jesus' third birthday, never rich in material things but wealthy beyond measure with their abundant love for each other and the One Most High.

They developed a routine of prayers, work, and rest. But even on the darkest days, they found something for which they could be joyful. Rachel gave birth to a baby girl they named Ruth, and the two families joined as one in their work, play, and prayer.

From season to season, from flood to bountiful crops, hot days to chilly nights, their lives in service to God continued.

On a night dark except for the twinkling of stars in the vast, deep sky, the family finished their evening meal and gathered to offer their evening prayer. Joseph sat on a cushion at the head of the table with Mary to his right and Nur to his left. Jesus sat beside Nur, holding his hand; the others were also seated there. With their heads bowed and hands joined together, Joseph opened their prayer, "Our Heavenly Father…"

Without warning, a mighty wind roared into the house even though there were no storm clouds in the area. The howling gusts drowned out their prayer and blew out both candles illuminating the room.

In the sudden darkness, Nur stiffened. The image appeared as it had so many years ago, standing behind Joseph. Nur, now a young man, had seen it previously when God's messenger delivered the ominous warning of Herod's evil intent. Tonight he heard the same quiet voice, but this time with a message of ebullience that only Nur heard. Upon receiving the joyful words, Jesus' brother closed his eyes, his heart pounding in his chest.

The wind stopped as unexpectedly as when it had rushed upon them. The candles flickered anew, and the room reclaimed its calming radiance.

Still holding Jesus' hand, Nur looked to Joseph and Mary, then to baby Ruth and her parents. Tears flowed down his cheeks. His voice quaked when he spoke. "Herod is dead. We can return home!"

Chapter Nine
Jerusalem

Joseph, always the organized and meticulous leader of the household, set about preparing for what he considered the ultimate gift from God—to deliver the Redeemer to His home in Israel. He coordinated tasks between himself, Nadab, and Nur: plan and prioritize their schedule to determine what *must* be taken home versus what they would *like* to take, establish prices for items they might be able to sell, set aside objects they would donate to the poor, and physically prepare themselves and their donkeys for the arduous trip home.

Aware of the donkeys' limitations in the rigors of the Negev, he planned to improve his lot as much as possible within their limited means. When the preparations were nearing completion, he visited merchants, Bedouins, and Nabataeans to purchase a one-hump dromedary. The expense of the animal, while depleting their meager savings, would be a worthy investment for the challenges that lay ahead in crossing the desert. The local citizenry took advantage of the family and paid little for their hard-earned possessions. Nevertheless, with negotiations and payments complete, the two families prepared for the journey that would forever change human history. Within the week, Joseph had completed an exchange of goods and money with a young Bedouin—now they owned a camel.

That night he stood beside the stone corral that held the donkeys and the camel, absorbing the stillness of the evening. The moon rose over the horizon, creating a medley of stars and planets set against the splendor of the full moon. A soft and sweet breeze swept across the river. Joseph's heart and soul were at peace. The Eighth Psalm reigned in his mind:

"When I behold Your heavens, the work of Your fingers, the moon and the stars which You have set in place—What is man that You are mindful of him? You made him a little lower than the angels. You crowned him with glory and honor."

Joseph took a deep breath and turned toward the animals that would carry them across the desert and home. He chuckled as the jenny stuck its nose into his face. He stepped back slightly, then petted its nose and ears. Joseph felt a special fondness for this little animal. They had been through so much over the years, but now their homeland awaited them. With faith in the Almighty, they had prepared spiritually and physically as best they could.

The next day he learned of a caravan going to Jerusalem and Damascus. He wasted no time in arranging passage with the caravan master. When the new day dawned, they would once again cross the desert—this time to home with a new life awaiting them.

Rising before the sun crested the distant hills, they concluded their last-minute packing, loaded the animals, and joined the merchants' camp across the river. The caravan boasted a dozen donkeys and a hundred dromedaries, with an equal number of men employed as camel pullers. Each animal carried a load of linens, fine oils, jewelry, precious stones, and intricate wood and ivory carvings. Such treasures would be tempting prey for thieves, but the sizeable traveling party assured them safety.

The caravan moved steadily, breaking camp before dawn and moving until the heat of the day, resting beneath tents until the blazing sun receded into the horizon, then continuing until darkness overtook them. They set up a camp for the evening when they came to an oasis. Otherwise, they moved on, setting up a dry camp when necessary.

Nur balanced his work time between the women and children, the men, and the donkeys and camel. The dust from the animals' hooves and the travelers' feet created a thick, sandy cloud through which they walked all day. Their eyes and noses dried in the heat and dust, and their lips cracked from the lack of moisture, but they did not complain. Soon enough, they would be home with their families, enjoy good shelter, and have ample food and drink, beds for the children, and the temple in which they would praise God Almighty.

They gave thanks daily for the privilege of the journey, grateful for the blessings the Lord bestowed on them. When they reached Jerusalem, they stayed once again in the house where they'd found shelter before the flight into Egypt. After one night's rest, Joseph and his family moved northward without the caravan while others moved toward their destinations.

Homeward bound, the little entourage moved more quickly than when they'd begun their trip for the census. At Joseph's behest, Nur, now a mature young man, detoured to Nazareth to proclaim the good news to Joachim and Anne.

The grandparents began preparing the young family's home for their joyous return. By the time the two families would reach Nain, Joachim and Anne would have the house cleaned throughout, refreshed with the scent of candles and flowers, and well stocked with life's necessities.

Anne filled packs of fruit and bread, jugs of good wine, oil for their lamps, blankets, linens, and fresh clothes. Joachim gathered chisels, hammers, and more tools for Joseph to re-establish himself in his trades of carpentry and masonry. They carried all they could and would have given all they owned to reunite with their daughter, her husband, and the child, Jesus—the Messiah. Together, they would nurture the Son of God and bear witness to His holy works. They didn't know what to expect, but they would share whatever God allowed.

Before the last rays of the sun flickered on the horizon of the seventh day, Joseph and his family reached the safety and comfort of their home. They left as three but returned as seven—two families filled with the love of God embedded in their souls.

Rachel and Nadab returned to Joachim's household, leaving Mary with Jesus, Joseph, and Nur at their home. With the new tools he received from Joachim, Joseph restored the house with fresh stucco, planted crops, pruned and fertilized his grove, and built screens in the house to provide privacy for his wife and child.

Mary cared for Jesus and maintained the home while Nur worked with both wherever his services were in demand.

Joseph and Nur slept in the main room on mats they kept rolled into the corner during the day, while Mary and Jesus slept in their private area.

Dining took place at a low table in the main room, while the cooking occurred in a *tannur* and fire pit in the courtyard.

Joseph had built their latrine outside the compound walls, away from the spring, but pleasingly surrounded by oleander bushes blooming in the warmth of the seasons.

They started each day the same, rising at the sound of the first cock. While Jesus slept, the others gathered for prayer and reflection. Then Mary prepared the morning meal while Nur and Joseph readied for their chores. Joseph usually worked on projects he had taken on from various small businesses and farms. At the same time, Nur cared for the animals and crops. After Mary prepared the meal and Jesus roused from His sleep, they gathered for prayer to God, asking for His blessings upon them.

Jesus, still a little boy, spent the days following His mother around the house, chasing chickens through the field, trying to catch young lambs, or finding a place to nap. He often either wanted to eat at an odd hour or refused to eat when mealtime arrived.

Mary sometimes wondered if she had been a worthy mother for the child of God. Had she been weak or doubtful? Hesitant, or dubious? Indeed, she sometimes questioned herself as a faithful servant of God. Nevertheless, the days moved into weeks and the weeks into months. The child Jesus and His brother Nur grew in stature and maturity. And, too, Mary grew in confidence and grace.

With Joseph's permission, Nur built a one-room structure near the spring. He gathered limestone for the walls and the best-worked timbers for the roof. He added strips of wood to the edge of the thatched roof to funnel the rare rainfall into a small cistern. Then, he built an ornate altar using *nophek* (turquoise) nuggets, stones, and old timbers. He purchased brass oil lamps in Nazareth with money for piecework he did for neighbors, then placed them on the altar.

Having learned from his father, he took careful measurements, then built a window in the east wall so the rising sun would cast its glow directly on the altar on the first day of spring. To complete his efforts, he built another window in the west wall to allow the setting sun to bathe the altar at day's end.

Nur sometimes traded his labor to a merchant or family friend in Nazareth. In exchange for his work, he received four fine rugs, each colored deep red and purple and trimmed with elaborate white and yellow threads. He placed them on the floor of the oratory so he and the others would have a comfortable place to pray. Afterward, he and Joseph built two benches and put them against the back wall. Using pieces of wood left over from Joseph's work, the aspiring young carpenter built a modest tabernacle and placed it in the center of the altar. Inside, he put a scroll of Scripture given to him by Joachim.

Mary and Jesus often visited the oratory in the heat of the afternoon. With a good breeze wafting through the windows, they spent many afternoons in prayer. Many times, Jesus fell asleep in these comfortable settings on His mother's lap.

As Jesus grew in age and wisdom, He often visited the oratory and opened His heart and soul to His Father. His family watched Him grow in grace and understanding, exceeding that of any other young man.

Mary realized the oratory served as a holy place, so she beautified the path leading to it with cuttings from her rose bushes. It surprised her how quickly they flourished with their brilliant red colors and sweet scent brightening the spirituality of the house of prayer.

By the time Jesus achieved the age of ten, Nur had grown into a tall young man who, for his age, excelled in the art and science of carpentry and masonry. Merchants and wealthy men from Nazareth often sought his stylish touch for their homes or businesses, and he relieved Joseph of some of the heavy labor.

One afternoon a man and his young sons came to negotiate with Joseph and Nur about building cabinets and tables for their new home. The three adults sat in the shade of a pergola to discuss the job and settle on a fair price for the work. Jesus went with the two boys to the spring to play. Nur watched them as they took turns tossing a gourd over the spring into a wicker basket on the other side.

Their business complete, Joseph and the man walked toward the front gate while Nur went to tell the boys their father had completed his business. Just then, the older of the two boys missed catching the gourd, and in frustration, kicked the gourd solidly. It struck a rose bush and broke off a branch. The broken piece slapped against Jesus' cheek and forehead where He stood near the spring. The thorns pricked Him, and He moaned, frightening the other boys. They ran away but did not tell their father or Joseph what had happened.

Nur hurried to His aid, knelt beside Him, and comforted Him as he picked out the thorns. Blood spurted down His forehead and dripped off the tip of His nose when Nur removed the thorn, but instead of crying, Jesus grimaced and held His breath and His tears.

"They meant no harm," Nur said, pressing against the wound with the hem of his shirt.

"I know," Jesus whispered as He watched the blood drip into the water, where it washed down the hill to the trees in the grove. Jesus continued, "There will be another day when thorns will pierce My flesh, My blood will flow into the ground, and as this water flows to nourish the trees, My blood will flow to nourish souls for the Kingdom of Heaven."

Nur nodded his understanding. "I assure You whatever shall come, I will guard You as much as our Father in heaven allows. A day will come that You and our father are no longer with our mother, but I shall stand beside her forever. I love her with eternal love as every child should love his mother."

Jesus and his older brother exchanged glances as they had years ago during Jesus' infancy. Once again, each understood the other.

Chapter Ten
Lost

As they did each year at Passover, the family journeyed to Jerusalem to celebrate the feast beginning at sunset on the fourteenth day of *Nisan* (springtime). After Passover and following social norms, they started the homeward-bound trek. All males at least twelve years old traveled together. Women traveled with the children, and with Jesus being twelve years old, Mary assumed He accompanied Joseph and Nur.

Typically, Joseph and Mary, as did most families, joined each other for the evening meal at the end of the day. When they gathered at the appointed time and place, Mary found her husband and did a quick visual search for Jesus. Not seeing Him, she looked sternly at Joseph. "Where is Jesus?" she snapped.

Joseph scanned the crowds of people before he caught Mary's eyes. "I assumed He would be with you," he replied, cupping her hands in his. "Pray, my love. God has not abandoned us. That we know." He forced a smile and spoke confidently. "We will find Him."

Looking about, Mary saw Nur on the hillside gathering wood and chips for a fire. She frantically ran to him, shouting, "Nur, where is Jesus? Is He not with you?"

"We were ready to leave," he said while tucking the firewood into the crook of his arms. "He told me to go with you and Joseph and He would be with us soon."

With her voice pitched and eyes wide with anxiety, she spoke sharply. "Where did you leave Him?"

Nur's voice and demeanor were calm and confident when he spoke. "At the wall near the gate. He told me it was not yet time. 'Be of no concern for Me,' He commanded, Mother. I encouraged Him to come, but He said for me to say nothing until you inquired."

Mary's voice carried a tinge of stress and anxiety. Beads of sweat dotted her brow as she spouted out a litany of questions. "What did He plan to do? Why couldn't He come with us? Why would He worry us like this?"

"Mother," Nur said, "He told me the day would come when He would be about His mission and that I should be there for you. Nothing more."

"Tomorrow, we go back," she replied. Her demeanor subsided, her voice strong and motherly.

They searched throughout the old city. Finally, on the third day, they found Jesus in the temple in discourse with grown men, listening to them, asking them questions, and enjoying conversation with them.

Nur stood with Joseph and Mary near the temple doors, observing and listening to the dialogue.

The men spoke with Him as if He were one of them, learning from Him as He did from them.

Mary took Joseph's hands and clasped them in hers, holding her husband to give her strength, for she understood the immensity of Jesus' mission. More so, she understood the joy and sorrow that would come to her through her Son.

When Jesus and the men's conversation began to fade, He turned slowly toward His family. Without smiling, and with the slightest nod of His head, the Son of God acknowledged His family. He rose from the bench upon which He rested and walked to the rear, where He embraced His mother, then His father and brother.

He began to speak, but Mary interrupted and admonished Him for causing her distress. Her mood and voice were patient yet manifested the anguish she and Joseph had undergone.

Her divine Son listened obediently, then again embraced His mother. "Mother, do you not know I must be about my Father's business?"

Mary shuddered as the power of the Most High embraced every fiber of her being. Knowingly, Jesus held her hand while the family exited the temple. Nur followed behind when they went down the steps. In doing so, he allowed his heart and soul to grasp the growth of the Son of God—a young man and the divine manifestation of the Almighty. A smile crept across his face as he further understood *his* mission to be a servant to the Holy Family.

Jesus grew into a strong young man, standing at least as tall as Joseph, broad in the shoulders with long, curly hair flowing to the nape of His neck. Wisps of a beard grew on His chin, just enough to make Him the target of good-natured joking from His friends.

Mary thought Him handsome, if not a magnificent young man. He worked hard under His father's tutelage, gaining skills in carpentry and negotiating prices for the items they built or repaired.

Shortly after He turned twenty-six years old, Jesus invited Nur to go into Nazareth with Him to buy household items for their mother. They traveled on a cold and foggy morning, wearing robes over their inner garments with mantles draped over their heads. The bleak, damp weather caused most people to stay home, so the two young men at least had the pleasure of enjoying the empty road. The fog dropped lower and lower, blanketing the rocky hills and wrapping the two travelers in a shroud of mist.

Jesus held His wrap to His face as he turned to speak. "Nur, My brother, we have been together for many years. I asked you to come today so we can talk privately."

Nur responded with a quizzical look in his eyes. "Of what do You speak, little brother?"

Jesus walked silently for a few steps, kicked a pebble down the road, then pulled His garments tighter against the cold, damp air. "The day has not yet come that I should leave to follow My Father's commands. Still, I must go so I can learn of the cultures, the mores and taboos, the things that are important to all people—men and women, Jews and gentiles, to people of this land and foreigners, people of our race and others." He paused and caught his breath against the cold, then continued. "Each person is different, yet each is the same because all are My Father's children. I must know them better. Only then can I kiss my parents goodbye and set forth on my life's mission." He took another deep breath, exhaled, and watched his breath in the cold air. "The time for Me to learn has arrived. Nur, will you come with Me? Will you continue to be My elder brother? My guardian? The one who shall light the pathway?"

Nur stopped in his tracks, grabbed his brother's arm, and pulled Him to a standstill. With his hands on Jesus' shoulders, he looked deeply into the Messiah's eyes. Time and the world froze, then Nur spoke. "I will be where our Father commands. With you, our family, or wherever I am needed." He paused, took a deep breath, and exhaled slowly while still grasping his brother. "I know You are the Son of God, and I will do all that should be done. The command I received is always to be there because You are my Lord."

"Then so be it," Jesus replied. "We shall get the things for our mother, and tonight after prayer, I will tell them."

"And when exactly will we leave?"

"We'll help father prepare for the coming winter and then be on our way. We will go north to Capernaum where we will work with fishermen, and then to the Great Sea. We will work north, earning our way as carpenters, fishermen, or field servants. Each day we will learn from those around us. We will learn what is important to them and what is not. We will learn of their beliefs and faith in our Father, but we will do so quietly, for it is not yet time for Me to do more."

⚜

They entered the city and went to the well where they found a fire that others had made. They slipped in and warmed their hands over the blaze after two young boys scooted aside to make room for them. Rubbing his hands together, Nur glanced at Jesus and asked, "There is more, is there not?"

"Yes, much more. So much that I find it hard to describe." Jesus was deep in thought while He watched the flames lick the wood in the fire pit. He hesitated, then continued. "We will hire ourselves onto a ship at Tyre or Sidon. They always need carpenters when they are underway, and our father taught us excellent skills. We'll go to lands we have never seen—to Antioch and Myra, then on to Ephesus and Corinth." He looked at Nur through the smoke and heat waves and offered a comforting smile. "Yes, it is a long way, but we can do it, and we'll learn so much. Then, and only then, can I be about My Father's commands."

"Why these particular places?" Nur asked.

"Except for one, we are to learn from the people." He paused and looked through the spiral of smoke rising from the fire. "To that *one,* we go because that is where our mother will live out her last days, and you will be at her side."

The two brothers fell silent. Once again, they exchanged a spiritual relationship unseen by the human eye, and Nur understood.

Tears welled in Jesus' eyes. "My brother, many will care for our mother, but you will be the one closest to her heart. Her life will be one of love and torment. However, she will always be at peace in her soul. You shall be with her forever and give her comfort before she leaves that place to go to her heavenly reward."

"Where are you talking about?"

"Ephesus! There you and she will find friends and believers who will comfort her, even though most Ephesians will not know My Father or Me."

They left the fire's warmth and made their purchases in near silence. The land remained blanketed in a cold mist when they began the long walk home, each lugging a bundle over their shoulders. They were well on their way before Nur spoke. His teeth chattered, not so much from the weather, but from the thoughts that raced through his mind. "I tremble, Jesus. It is more than this miserable season. It is my heart. It is full of sorrow and joy, and I don't know how to explain it."

Jesus looked from beneath the shroud He had pulled around His face and grinned at His brother. "You are my older brother. Are you not supposed to explain these things to Me?"

The two young men looked at each other and laughed. Despite the divinity of God-made-man, they could get a good laugh from one another.

They pulled their wraps tightly against the weather before Jesus commented again. He had a slight smirk in His voice. "At least we can keep our heads down out of the wind and not have to worry about bumping into someone or them running into us. We're the only ones foolish enough to go out in this weather."

The day of their departure arrived. Mary and Joseph walked with their sons—Mary's arm around Jesus' waist, Joseph's arm draped over Nur's shoulder. They stopped at the gate.

Joseph, with tear-filled eyes, looked deeply into Nur's eyes. "Remember, son. You are the '*Light of the Lord*.'" He took a deep breath and exhaled as tears cascaded through his greying beard. "You carry a heavy burden on your shoulders."

Nur's lips curled into a forced smile, but his eyes watered when he spoke. "I will never forget, Father. The yoke is light."

Both men turned at the sound of Mary's voice when she addressed her Son. "Jesus, our hearts are filled with the grace of God. Go forth as Your Father commands, knowing we will constantly pray for both of you." She kissed him on the cheek and stepped back as the two young men turned onto the roadway and began their journey.

Mary and Joseph stood proud but forlorn when they watched Jesus, the Messiah, and Nur, the lad of unknown origin, begin their trek to the Sea of Galilee.

Chapter Eleven
His Journey

The travelers each carried only a small pack on their belt with a plan to earn their food and lodging as they went. They traveled first to Cana, then on to Magdala, and finally to Capernaum, where they rested at the end of their third day's walk.

"Jesus," Nur asked, "why did we go in such a roundabout way to get here when we could have been here in only two days?"

"Remember," Jesus said, "we come to learn, not to run like children in a footrace. Did we not see a widow crying at the death of her husband in Cana? Did we not see the carpenter looking in vain for work in Magdala?" Jesus looked at His brother and smiled lovingly. "We must understand the difficulties—the stress, humiliation, loneliness, or the poverty people suffer daily. The widow is lost because she has no relatives to care for her. The young carpenter had no work for two days but cared for a wife and child. I must learn to understand these people fully if I am to serve them. That is why we are in no hurry to get anywhere."

"You said we would stay here in Capernaum and work. Why here and not elsewhere? Why did we not stay in those places to help them?"

"It is not yet time for Me to fulfill My mission, but the day will soon come when I will give My life for each of them. Now, though, we are here to learn what they find to be joyous or unpleasant. Only then can I complete the mission as instructed by God in heaven. Look about you." Jesus gestured with open arms at the multitude of people, shops, and boats tied to the wharves. "Men come here from every direction, by foot and by boat, because this is the best fishing in the whole area. Here we will see and learn, and here we will work among the people."

The two young men found food and lodging in exchange for helping a man mend his nets that had been torn on the rocks. He gave them old mats, which they rolled out in a shed at the fish store, a room with a strong odor, but out of the wind from the sea. The next day they went to the synagogue.

Nur took a seat near the door and observed when Jesus entered and began discussing the prophets' words with the rabbis and elders. He asked questions sincerely and with a certain degree of humility. They, in turn, answered Him with great pride, for it was unusual for a man of His age to show such depth and to have gained so much knowledge of the prophets and the rules set down many years ago. The morning passed quickly, and the men invited Jesus to return the next day, for they found satisfaction with His company and interest.

"You have a good future, young man," an elder said. "Follow our guidance, and we will show you the gates of heaven. You are an intelligent person. You can live well, and the people will treat you with high esteem."

Jesus and Nur stayed in Capernaum for three months. They found permanent lodging in an outbuilding that two brothers and their widowed mother owned. In exchange for tending the brothers' nets and repairing their boats which the wind occasionally bounced off the rocky shore, the travelers also were given a morning and evening meal for their work. Each morning, the fishermen left before sunrise. Jesus and Nur met them upon their return and readied the boat and nets for the next day.

The two fishermen sold their abundant catch each evening and were pleased with the new leisure time to care for their mother. The exchange of labor satisfied all of them.

Jesus went to the synagogue almost every day where the rabbi and the elders relished His company, learning and teaching with and from Him.

An old woman who tended the linens in the synagogue asked Jesus why He visited Capernaum. "If you and Nur are the sons of Joseph of Nazareth, why are you not there with your father instead of here talking all the time?"

Jesus replied, "Here men and women from all regions come to buy fish or to shop in the merchants' stalls. My Father directed Me to come to this land to learn from you, so when I go about His work, I will be familiar with people's habits, their wants and needs, and how I can best meet their wishes. When I know this, then I will be able to serve them."

"Well," she replied, "Your father is very indulgent. I think you should be working with him. After all, you will be a carpenter. What else do you need to know to do that?"

Jesus smiled at her and accepted her criticism, knowing she was unaware of the true meaning of His Father's work.

Chapter Twelve
Capernaum

Sunrise painted swaths of pink and blue across the sky. Shading His eyes from the glare, Jesus paused to enjoy the few moments of the beauty of God's handiwork. He chuckled under His breath. Could His Father haven been playing and having fun when He painted it?

Ready to resume their journey, He roused Nur from his sleep with a gentle tug on the shoulder accompanied by a soft, "It is time, Nur. We must go."

Nur rolled over, squinting and rubbing his eyes. "Jesus, is there no limit to Your energy? Don't we need to sleep a little longer?"

Jesus flipped the blanket back and jostled his brother's streaking grey and brown hair. "Did Abraham not rise early and go on his way?" Without waiting for a response, He continued. "As did our forefathers, we too must rise and be on our way."

Nur gave a muffled groan and yawn, rose from his mat, and stretched. With a heartfelt smile creasing his lips, he commented, "Jesus, while my body may tire out, my soul is encompassed with the spirit of our Holy Father. Let us pause and give praise to Him. Then, let us be on our way."

After their morning routine, they strapped on their sandals, grabbed their bundles of clothes, and tossed them over their shoulders. Setting out from Capernaum, they bade goodbye to their newly found friends and began their walk up the face of the steep, rocky incline and away from the city. They quickly found the well-used pathway to be a challenging series of switchbacks and scree, making it even more difficult with the morning sun glaring into their eyes.

The sun reached a high point in the sky before they reached the mountain crest and paused to catch their breath. Capernaum had treated them well. It served to be a welcoming environment where people came from throughout the distant lands.

Schools of fish swam among the rocks where a skilled fisherman could fill his nets with enough to feed his family and have an ample supply to sell in the marketplace. Bountiful streams and rivulets drained from the distant hills and mountains, joining together on the rocky shores of the Sea of Galilee, replenishing the water into the deep.

Jesus sat on the edge of the bluff overlooking the city, taking in the panoramic view. With His cloak flapping in the wind, He wrapped a stole over His forehead to shield Himself from the scorching heat. In the city below, He observed travelers coming from all directions, some on foot and others riding donkeys and camels.

Nur sat beside Him while they observed the activity in the city and the boats working the shoreline. "They are strong and skilled young men," Nur said as they watched the men steer their craft carefully along the coastline, rolling in the greenish-blue swells and casting their nets between the rocks.

"The sea is a gift from the Father," Jesus replied, "delivering an abundance of life where men come from afar to partake of its riches. The city, with its shopkeepers and buyers, is another of His limitless gifts. Just look as men and women bustle about through the streets and alleys. It is a wonderful sight." He smiled when He caught Nur's eye. "Capernaum is a natural setting for the work of God. Whatever a person needs can be found there." Rising from the rock on which they had rested, Jesus looked over His shoulder at Nur and spoke solemnly. "I shall return here to fulfill the work of My Father, for here the rivers of life come together. And too, I shall gather men into My Father's house here."

Nur grimaced, his face stung by the wind, as the gusts had nearly drowned out Jesus' voice.

"Capernaum is a beautiful setting, here at the foot of this rocky escarpment and the headwaters of the sea. This is where men, women, and children find the quality of life. It is Capernaum where they find food for their bodies, and here they shall find food for their souls.

"There shall be another location far from this land. Another place where the waters flow and men gather." He glanced at Nur, then back to the city. "No Roman, gentile, or Jew has seen it—only My Father. Men of a primitive life will establish it and call it home. The name they will give it is *Bac* because, in their language, that is a place where the waters gather. Those who hear My Word and believe in Me shall go there and tell the people of My Father. Then, they too will believe."

He stepped to the edge of the precipice, spread his arms, and spoke in a voice that pierced the elements. "They shall build a great house of prayer, a White Dove in the Desert, and it will stand until the end of time, for My Father's Word cannot die."

Nur fell to his knees in prayer. The power of the Lord overwhelmed him.

In the city below and the boats upon the sea, everyone heard the voice of the Messiah like the clang of a bell shattering the midnight quiet. They didn't know its origin, but at that moment, fish overwhelmed the fishermen's nets and milk filled the withered breasts of mothers.

Jesus tightened the belt around His waist and walked, taking the first of many steps that would continue for two years through arid desert, across verdant mountains, and onto the high seas. They would share the joys and sorrows that men, women, and children experience. They would eat when they worked. Otherwise, they would sleep on empty stomachs. Their lives would mirror those of other people. They would live among God's children, learning the triumphs and tragedies of all peoples without favor or subjugation.

They traveled until late afternoon of the first day, finally arriving at a scattering of houses and fruitful fields high in the green hills and valleys northwest of Capernaum. They smelled smoke long before the winding trail led them over the top of the highest ridge. From here, they saw the last flickers of a fire burning a man's vineyard.

Jesus pointed toward several men struggling to smother the flames. "Let's see if we can help them." They ran the remaining distance down the path to the vineyard.

Gasping for breath, Nur asked a young man holding a burned and battered rag he had been using to extinguish the fire, "May we help?"

The vineyard keeper looked at them, his face blackened with ash. "You are too late," he said as he looked at the remains of his field. "The gods have not been with me this year." He yanked the roots of a withered vine from the ground. "Nothing! Nothing!" he bellowed, throwing it down. "All of this work for nothing!"

He wiped the grime from his face with his sleeve and plodded toward his house on the hillside above the vineyard. The other men picked up their tools and walked away quietly, leaving the young man alone in his misery.

Jesus and Nur watched silently as the man went to his home where his wife and a small child stood in the doorway. The woman took her husband's hand and led him into the house, leaving the youngster to sit in the doorway.

"I have an idea," Nur said when he stepped over the scree in the trail and began walking toward the house. "Come with me, Jesus," he coaxed. "I have seen this done before."

"What do you have in mind, or have you lost your mind?" Jesus teased.

Nur looked over his shoulder and nodded. "Come and see."

At the house, the brothers called out to the man who came to the door, downcast and dirty.

"Listen, my friend," Nur said. "We are strangers to this land in need of food and shelter. We will work for you, asking only to sleep in your stable and share your food."

"My friends! You can see I have lost everything. How do you expect me to give you jobs?"

"Look," said Nur, scraping the burnt bark off one of the vines. "The fire spread quickly, but neither too hot nor too deep." He broke off a portion of the vine, showing it to the young man. "See, only the outer part of the vine and the leaves are burnt, but the heart and the roots of the vine are still good. They live." He handed the vine to the man. "We can return your vineyard to its finest day, I am sure. I have seen it done before, and we can do it again."

The man looked at his new friends and smiled. "I believe, sir, you are right." He called his wife who came to the door. She stooped and lifted the child to her bosom as her husband introduced them. "My name is Micah," he said as he reached his hand to his new friends, "and this is my wife, Mahlah." He tousled the hair of his child and continued. "The little one is Ahaz." He looked at Jesus and Nur as he continued. "You are welcome to stay with us, and all we have is yours. I can never express to you how much I appreciate your help."

Jesus and Nur spent two full months working with Micah, pruning the burned branches and leaves from the vines, separating the thriving plants from those too flawed to be saved. The useless plants were bundled and cast into a fire. In the end, it would produce a masterful white wine.

To enrich the healthy plants, the men worked from early morning until nightfall, scooping a shallow ditch around each plant where the *vigneron* could bring the waters of temporal life to them. Only when the land flourished and the plants were healthy did the two men leave Micah and his family and continue their journey.

They paused on the ridge overlooking the vineyard, its plants showing signs of new life. Jesus looked at His callused and blistered hands. "For sure, My brother, we have learned how hard it is to grow grapes."

Nur laughed. "I will appreciate wine even more now. Being a vigneron is harder than I thought it would be, and overhauling irrigation systems is more difficult than I anticipated. I thought we might work the skin off our bones!"

"And what did we learn?" Jesus inquired.

Nur looked over his shoulder at Jesus as they walked. "Be careful with fire," he joked.

Jesus chuckled as He picked up His staff and fell in behind Nur, walking again toward the desert and the Great Sea.

"Nur," Jesus said, "Mother repeated the story many times over these years of how you led the way to Bethlehem and later to Egypt. She said that sometimes her rational mind would question where you were taking them, but her faith never faltered. And neither does Mine. You are a great companion." He tousled Nur's hair and joked, "The times haven't changed a bit, have they? You still lead as you are destined to do."

Nur maintained a steady pace, going uphill or downhill, on good highways or precarious trails. He was vigilant about obstacles or hazards, always planning how far they needed to go to find rest and shelter for the night and deciding whether to increase or slow their gait. As he had done for many years, he saw his charge to care for the Messiah as one of unlimited joy. Neither the hottest day, the coldest night, nor the steepest trail daunted him. He would lead the Son of God to the ends of the earth. Of that, he had no doubt.

Their journey led them over the mountains and into the desert, through cities growing in population and importance and others that were the remnants of once-great cities. They worked and lived as carpenters, field laborers, and shepherds, often doing meager labor for a pittance. On many days they earned only enough money to buy food to live on until the next workday, but on others, they worked for kind and generous men who paid them well. They traveled through locales such as Ramah, Janoah, and numerous scattered settlements and unnamed villages.

After four months, they came to the desert near Beth-Emek. They decided to rest and work only sporadically but catch up on their sleep, taking time to let their legs rest from the distance they had covered in the weeks since they left home. Here, Jesus found a kind old gentleman who agreed to make new sandals for them in exchange for repairing his creaky and crumbling old house.

Talking to the old man by the fire one night, they learned to know him as Zaida, which meant "elderly person" or "grandfather." His actual name was Jechonias, and he had been born of the lineage of the house of David and, therefore, maintained a blood relationship with Jesus.

Jechonias said when he was a young married man, he and his family were sold into slavery by nomadic tribesmen who took them prisoner after raiding a caravan. "We spent years in bondage. Our masters sold me time after time until I lost all hope of ever finding my family. I have not seen my wife and children in more than twenty years. I went free after a wealthy landowner bought me for my skill as a leathersmith. I remained faithful to him for many years, and for that, he freed me. Now, I am alone."

His voice quaked with anger. He paused, picked up a rock, and bashed it into the fire. "Children and grown men make fun of me. They chastise me for my humped back and my stupid little gait, but I cannot help it. I used to be strong and agile, but not always like this. But I suffered so many whippings and beatings that I became little more than a shadow of my former self. I ate only what I could purchase on the measly earnings I received from an occasional farmer or shopkeeper. When that did not feed me, I sat beside the roadway and begged—not much pleasure for a man who had everything," he muttered.

Jesus and Nur saw a tear in his eye before he wiped it out with his gritty finger.

"I had a good business, and people came from far away to have me work for them. I was good...very good," he said proudly. Then he pointed toward the hills. "But those bastards stole it all from me. My wife, my children, everything."

He looked at his new friends. "It's not often I have someone to talk with. I appreciate your willingness to listen to an old man grumble." He hunched his shoulders and gave a humiliated grin. "You're not here to spy on me, are you? Did somebody send you to get me? I cannot trust many people these days, you know."

"No," Nur said. "We are not spies, just men looking for a place to rest and work."

"Good, because what I say is blasphemy." He looked around at the growing darkness for assurance they were alone. "We all know there is supposed to be a God, but I'm starting to question His existence. A good God doesn't let this happen to a family man. No. A good God would never do that, so I have my doubts."

He studied them and tried to judge their reactions, but they only warmed their hands by the fire and offered a reassuring smile to him.

"Tell me, if there really is a God, why would He let my family be destroyed? You tell me why . . ." His voice trailed off, his body shook, and tears flowed freely from his tired old eyes. After a few minutes, he got up to go into his house. "I'm weary, my friends. I need to sleep."

Jesus and Nur watched the old man go to his cramped little room at the back of the building. They sat silently for a few minutes, watching the fire die before going in and laying out two worn, tattered old mats Jechonias had given them.

Jesus took off his sandals and lay down in the corner. He looked up at Nur, who hesitated.

"Lie down," Jesus said. "Go to sleep."

But Nur sat, his mat pushed aside. He could not decide whether he wanted to sleep.

"What is it?" Jesus whispered.

Nur bit his lip and shook his head. "I have never heard anybody say anything like that. Blasphemy, that's what it is. How can you sleep after hearing him make such indecent comments? How can we stay in this house?" He shrugged, surrendered to exhaustion, and stretched out on his mat, his movements manifesting his disgust when he kicked his sandals off and threw aside his little bundle of personal possessions.

Jesus leaned over him and whispered, "How can we judge him, Nur? Look what he has been through. We know a truth that has not yet been revealed to him." From the darkness of the back room came the sound of the old man breathing deeply. He began snoring and gasping as though he had forgotten to breathe.

Jesus smiled, then whispered, "Let's go outside, Nur. What do you want to say?" Jesus asked as he pulled on his sandals.

They walked a short distance from the house, where they could talk without waking Jechonias.

Nur looked sternly at Jesus, his eyes raged, and his lips pursed. "Jesus, You are the Messiah, and this man blasphemes. We cannot stay, even if we must walk in the darkness of the night. We need to go *now*. I cannot allow the likes of this man to talk to You!"

"My brother, how can we feel what he feels? So many people have wronged him for so many years."

"I know, but he has a responsibility not to judge God but to live His commandments." Nur stood stiffly. "He curses Your Father."

"Yes, you are correct," Jesus said. "He curses My Father, but I do not judge him, and to you, I say this: Love and pray for him, but do not judge that man. All he had, he lost, even his wife and children. Love him as My Father loves him. Forgive him as My Father forgives him. But now, I am sleepy, and look at you. You look even more tired than I. Let's go to sleep." He kissed His brother on the cheek and led him back into the house.

The two young men returned to their mats but couldn't sleep because of Jechonias's raucous snoring coming from the other room.

Jesus gave a halfhearted chuckle and commented, "Anyone who snores that loud needs our prayers."

Nur gave a soft murmur, then pulled a blanket over his head and lay back, hoping for sleep to come quickly.

Chapter Thirteen
Jechonias

The brothers toiled for three months, making the old house habitable. They replaced the window frames, rebuilt the front door, strengthened the roof supports, and added a small vegetable garden at the side of the house. When they ran out of money to buy what they needed, they worked for others—sometimes planting, other times repairing a home or stable. On one occasion, they trekked into the mountains to fetch a load of timber to haul to the port city of Akko for a new fishing dock.

All the while, Jechonias worked at his leather business. He had few customers, but as the quality of his life improved, the number of customers increased. In his youth, he was well-skilled and held in high esteem. As the years of bondage and self-pity overcame him, the quality of his work diminished. While his life with Nur and Jesus continued, his daily life improved, as did his leatherwork. It became as good as it had been in his youth.

One day an old Bedouin surprised Jechonias. After hearing others speak of Zaida, the caravan leader traveled far off his appointed route to purchase harnesses for his camels. Jechonias never knew of a Bedouin buying from a Jew. Still, this desert traveler heard of him and walked many days with his camels for Jechonias to rig them with new bridles and reins. He had heard other Bedouins and even a few Jews talking about the old Jew called Zaida, the finest leatherworker in the land. The Bedouin had seen his work, the finely cured leather cut with a precision unmatched by a king's tailor. He knew of reins studded with silver and small brass bells dangling from the harness. No ordinary man could do such fine work. Even if he was a Jew, a bridle was a bridle, and the camel had no concern about who made it.

With Zaida talking in Aramaic and the Bedouin speaking the Badawi language, they could communicate because they spoke a common language—a dialect of animals and leather. From that common point, the two old men set aside their differences for what they both needed, a transaction of bridles, reins, and trinkets. The Bedouin's visit brought Jechonias the realization that he had been reborn, not in the spiritual sense, but in the temporal, material world of mankind.

Jechonias enjoyed his new life. He shared his meals with friends and sold his sandals, belts, harnesses, and even chairs to many buyers. His house became a home filled with hard work, laughter, and companionship. Abundant food filled his belly. Best of all, he felt the sweet freshness of freedom and being in charge of his own life. Thanks to these two young men, he could live again. He could not replace the lost family or the spent years, but his mind and body renewed with an invigorating spirit.

While the freshly planted garden sprouted life from seeds, his personal life brought forth a new being—a man of age and wisdom, skill and good humor, compassion, and business sense.

However, Nur saw what Jechonias lacked. He found a new beginning without God, even though he had loved and adored God in his earlier years. The decades of slavery had robbed him not only of his family, but of his God. Nur questioned the price of Jechonias's new happiness.

Jesus and Nur often prayed for him, but one day decided their work with Jechonias was complete. They must continue with their journey.

After their morning meal of cheese, bread, and fresh figs, Jesus said to Jechonias, "We have enjoyed being with you these many days, but the time has come for us to move on." He put His arm around the old man's shoulders. "You are a kind and gentle man, my friend. You have found happiness again, and I thank you for allowing us to share these days with you."

"Oh no," Jechonias said. "I thank you and Nur." Jechonias took Jesus' hand and cupped it in his own. "My friends," he said as he glanced from Jesus to Nur, "it is you who have given me life, one I long ago surrendered to evil spirits." He reached out for Nur, now holding the hands of both of his friends. "I was lost, but you found me and gave me life, even more than I ever thought I would have."

"What do you mean?" Nur asked.

Jechonias chuckled. "We old folks don't sleep too well through the night—have to pee, you know. A couple of times, I got up, but you were not on your mats, so I went outside and found you down the path on your knees. I saw you on that hard, cold ground, your head bowed and your arms uplifted to heaven. I knew then that you were praying to your God and my God. I knew the first time I saw you in the darkness that I had been blind and deaf, but you opened my eyes and ears. You prayed for me, did you not?"

"Yes, my good friend," Nur replied. "Each of us prayed for you and everyone in the world so that all may know the one and only true God."

"I thank *you*, good sirs," Jechonias said. "I thank you with all my heart and soul. You have heard me say many terrible things, and I apologize to you and our God in heaven. From the point where the sun now stands, never again will I sin against God." The old man smiled, then took a jug of water from the mantel and shared it with them. "You poured out your lives for me as I poured out this water for your refreshment. Go forward in peace from this place, for you have shown me how to live as a man ought to live."

He bowed humbly to each of them. "Go in the name of God."

⚓

Jesus and Nur followed the highway along the coast, coming to the great port city of Tyre at nightfall on the third day. By far the biggest and most important city they visited, Tyre boasted a carnival-like atmosphere. All types of vendors packed the streets. Musicians played flutes and stringed instruments while children danced and played games in the common areas. Women baked bread and dried freshly caught fish from the Great Sea. Metalworkers hammered on brass and hot steel as they forged trinkets, bells, and swords.

The two brothers took in all the sights, sounds, and smells. They meandered through the twisting streets and alleys, finally exiting at the docks and wharves where ships great and small rested at moor. Jesus found them a place to sit on a wharf piling where they could enjoy the sights.

People of every nation assembled in this one place: Greeks and Romans, Turks and light-skinned people from the British Isles. Slaves and freemen worked side by side loading and unloading the cargo of every imagination—tin, wool, timber, dyes, fish, and the most pathetic of all matters for sale, men, women, and children, —enslaved people from lands far beyond the horizon. They were people from Asia and other distant nations who had been taken in battle and lost to a life of bondage.

"Is this where we should stay?" Nur asked. "Surely we can learn of every nation in this one place." He hopped up and chased away the gulls from a piling, then sat down as he took in the sights and sounds of the ships, their crews, and their cargoes. "Indeed," he commented, "this place is a sight to behold—so many people, so much to see. There is much for us to do here."

"No," Jesus said. "We will leave here shortly. As soon as we find a good ship with a good crew but in need of carpenters." He looked around at the ships in port and others coming and going on the horizon. "We have so much to see and learn and many places to go. We will rest here for a few days and offer prayer and thanksgiving to God for our safe journey, then join a crew and leave this place behind, never again to see it."

"Why?" Nur asked.

"For no greater reason than we must go to other places and learn of other people." Jesus rose and walked along the harbor, looking at the boats and enjoying the fresh salt breeze wafting across His face. "We could enjoy this place, no doubt. But we must move on, for the day will come when I shall be about My Father's mission." He casually glanced at Nur and continued. "We must not linger, for time is passing."

Along the water's edge, they found a lodge where other young Jews lived while they worked in the city. The house had many rooms and a common room where the woman proprietor provided the guests with an ample meal each morning. Nur paid her for the night's stay, and she led them down a hallway to a room with two cots and two jugs of fresh water on a table.

"Some people don't like this room because it's small, but it's my favorite because it's so quiet back here. You sleep without being disturbed. And look." She opened the drape over the window. "Keep this open, and you will get a good breeze."

"My lady," said Jesus, "tell me about the slaves. We saw so many of them."

"What can I tell you?" she asked. "They are like so many others. Some of them will live a hard life and die young." She shrugged her shoulders, as if helpless. "Others will have a life better than the one they left behind. Look at me. I lived as nothing more than a slave, but now I own my lodge and have a husband who owns a fishing boat. Not every slave owner is evil."

She poured them each a drink from a jug on a shelf. "They took me when I was a child. I worked for a Greek, and then a Turk stole me, but both treated me well. I cooked and cooked and cooked. Some days I thought I would die over a fire, but I always gave my masters what they wanted. I didn't steal from them and wouldn't tolerate those who did."

She walked to the window and looked out over the port. "It was right here in this city that I received my freedom. The old Turk had so much money he didn't know how to spend it. He had no family, and I cared for him as I would my own father."

She paused, staring into the distance, allowing the sweet ocean air to caress her face.

"His lungs gave out, and he died in his bedroom, but not before he freed every slave he owned." She faced the young men. Tears trickled down her cheeks. "He gave away everything he owned, his ship, his business, even this house." She shook her head, as if still not entirely understanding all that had happened to her. "He gave me this and gave his fishing boat to my husband, but we weren't married then. So you see, we ended up well."

"An amazing story," Nur replied.

"Life is strange. Hear it from an old woman. You never know who you will meet, so be careful. If you don't believe me, go to the temple and listen to them talk. A Messiah will come and free Israel. We don't know who He is or when He will come, but mark my word. The Messiah walks these lands as we speak, so live your lives accordingly. And now, my sweet guests, sleep well, for we know not what tomorrow will bring."

By mid-afternoon of the next day, Jesus and Nur found work on a Greek ship bound for Patara, a major port city in Lycia in Asia Minor. The trip would take them at least a week out of sight of land. The ship's Captain, Petropoulos, a lean, crusty man of Joseph's age, sought a skilled carpenter, for his ship was old though still seaworthy. He told his new crew the vessel was modeled after those of ancient times, but improvements to its structure gave it exceptional speed in good waters. Nevertheless, it drew little water compared to giant freighters that plied the sea. Its low-slung design made it vulnerable to strong winds or heavy swells that could move the ship far off course, causing it to lose whatever advantage its speed had given it.

He told them of a second weakness. The small ship had minimal cargo and crew space. However, its speed compensated for its smaller load capacity, giving it an edge over its larger competitors. To compete with the bigger vessels, this craft had to find good water and speed, which would make up for what it lacked in capacity, thus the need for a good carpenter. The ship had a single tier of seven oarsmen per side plus a tall single-masted sail. The mast and other parts suffered constant stress, and carpenters must be ready to repair or make new mast supports, yardarms, and oars throughout the day and night.

"The gods bless me," the Captain said. "We look and hope for good weather but never know what is beyond the horizon. Bad fortune in the way of storms, rains, and winds lie in wait to drag us to the bottom of the sea." He smirked, then gave them a sidelong glance. "I depend on Poseidon to guide us safely across these vast seas."

Taking a deep breath and stretching his back, he shifted the subject to the task at hand. "If you're as good as you say you are, you'll earn your pay. But you are young men without the feel of the sea beneath your feet. We will pitch and roll in the swells, and you will feel like a suckling with bad milk." He chuckled lightly and continued. "Rest well tonight because we sail with the morning tide. You may have to help the oarsmen sometimes, but you will find me a fair man. I will treat you well, but you must follow my orders without question, or you will never again see land. Am I understood?"

"Definitely," Nur replied. "We'll be here well before dawn, ready to sail."

Looking at the Captain, then at the workers loading the ship with its load of dried meats and fruits, Jesus said, "We'll serve you well, sir." He smiled. "As you say, we may spend some time hanging over the side until we get used to the ship's rolling and pitching."

"With good weather, we will be on the water and making speed, so you should do well," the captain said. "But if bad weather hits, we will roll so much that if you try to lean over the side, you may never come back up."

The ship slipped loose from its moorings with the morning tide. The smooth cadence of the oarsmen swiftly urged her away from the wharf, and in little time they were clear of the harbor, where a brisk breeze snapped the sail taut and pressed them into the open sea. As Petropoulos had said, the craft climbed atop the smooth waters, leaving the city's flickering lights in the darkness behind.

The two new crewmen busied themselves over the next several days repairing oars and oarlocks and an old rudder which they made better than new. At times, they took the oars and felt the power of the sea and winds work against them. Their backs strained and muscles cramped as they pulled the heavy oars through the slow-rolling water, keeping pace with the steady cadence of the ship's master, who banged out a resounding thump on an old drum. They took their turns at the dirty jobs of cleaning the sleeping quarters and eating utensils, plus emptying the slop pans into the water behind them. Nevertheless, they found amusement in watching the schools of fish sweep through the waste in search of tidbits to eat.

Shortly after sunset of the third night, the brothers sat near the small kettle heating soup for the crew's dinner, which Nur had prepared. He had carefully measured a portion of fresh water into a pot suspended over a metal plate upon which burning embers glowed. The water gradually began to simmer, and he tossed in onion, turnips, carrots, bits of garlic, and a small portion of salt. The meal would not be as tasty or nutritious as one his mother made, but would be hot and filling and give every man his fair share of what he needed to stay alive and work.

Petropoulos came out of his quarters. "I smell food." He smiled and sat next to Jesus, holding his hands to the warmth of the fire.

"Just getting started, Captain," Nur said as he stirred the soup with a spoon. "I think you will like this vegetable soup. When it's hot, I'll add some cheese to give it some body and a bit more taste." He shuddered with the damp chill of the ocean and pulled his tunic tight around his shoulders. "At least it won't kill you, I hope," he laughed.

"Too old and tough for that, my friend," Petropoulos said. "I'm not quite ready to cross the River Styx, but you believe differently, do you not?"

"Yes," replied Nur. "We believe there is but one Lord and God, the Master of love and forgiveness. He will take our souls to everlasting life in His heavenly kingdom if we have lived according to His commandments."

The three men sat in silence, watching the gentle glow of the embers as the soup heated.

"But you, Captain," inquired Nur, "you are a Greek and believe in many gods, do you not?"

Petropoulos chuckled, then spoke without taking his eyes from the embers. "Well, you poor devils only have one god, but I have many, so I'm bound to be better off. A god of the sea, another for speed, one for love, another one for power and might. I must be better off than you with only one god, and you cannot even see yours!" The captain held his hands close to the fire, rubbing them together against the cold sea air. "You put all your eggs in one basket and take too big of a chance, but that's your business, not mine. All I want from you is that you do your work. You can believe whatever you want."

Jesus leaned forward, putting his hands near the embers. "Tell Me, sir, if you will, about death and the afterlife as you believe it to be."

"I'll not match wits with you, Jesus, but I will tell you what I learned as a child."

The captain leaned forward, taking a small dagger from its sheath. He looked intently into the kettle, but doing more than selecting a vegetable to spear, he took time to calculate his response. Then, quick as lightning, he stabbed a carrot as it boiled to the top of the simmering pot. He blew on it to cool it, then popped it into his mouth, slowly chewing.

"As I learned as a child and still believe, when a person dies, whether man, woman, or child, he must cross the River Styx to reach paradise. Some will tell you different versions, but basically, they are all the same."

He leaned forward again, plucking another vegetable from the simmering water. "When a person dies, the soul inside him leaves the body and falls down the riverbank. You see," he looked first at Jesus and then at Nur, "the shore is nothing but slimy mud. It feels and smells like rotting death, or maybe the defecation of all who have gone before you. It is horrible. But the bank is so steep that you must pass it to get to the water's edge. The water, or as some say, the River Styx, is no better than the puke you're standing on: foamy brown and smells like death itself. Nothing is there—no fish, no weeds, no reeds. It's a place the gods forgot. Each person must cross the river by himself. If not, he must live for eternity in the slime and stench and dread of the riverbank. For each person, there is one raft and one raft only. Each must find his own and, with a pole, cross the river."

He shook his head, dreading the day he must endure the trial of the river.

"You don't know where to look or how far you must go to find your raft. Sometimes," he shuddered, "there are spirits there to guide you, but you don't know whether they're good or bad. They will tell you which way and how far you must go if they are good. If they are evil, they will lie to you, and you may never find your raft.

"It is critical for each person to lead a good life; if so, you won't have to deal with the evil spirits at the river's edge. Otherwise," he paused, "well, you can figure that out. As you cross over, the water improves. When you reach the opposite side, you find the purest water of all. That side is paradise."

"Is there a name for this paradise of yours?" Nur asked.

"The Elysian Fields. We must each endure a final test to reach the Elysian Fields—a paradise where we will live for eternity." He leaned forward, again looking into the bubbling kettle. "Do you intend to starve me and make me go to the River Styx tonight, or can we eat this potion of yours?" He laughed as he dipped a cup into the kettle.

Jesus stood watch at the helm throughout their seventh night at sea. The first hint of dawn stirred the horizon when He saw the faintest glimmer of lights. Patara lay directly ahead. By midmorning, they would reach the shore, then empty the ship of its cargo by late afternoon. They had completed their first voyage unscathed—no storms or sickness, no thieves or looters, no event that caused ill feelings or harm. The trip had been a journey of hard work, sweat, and modest meals, but nevertheless, a good experience.

"I will always remember this voyage," Jesus said to Petropoulos when they left the ship.

"I, too, young man," the captain replied. "I will remember you from this day forward." He looked over his shoulder at the sea and paused as if gathering his thoughts as he had the night when they sat around the simmering kettle. "Jesus, you and your brother are different from other men I have known. That troubles me, and I don't know why. I'm a judge of men, yet you chill my bones, which I cannot explain, but the day will come when I know what it is." He put a hand on each of their shoulders. "For now, travel well, my friends, and may the gods protect you until we meet again."

Chapter Fourteen
Ephesus

More than a year passed while Jesus and Nur ventured from Antioch to Rhodes, from Cnidus to Samos, on to Neapolis, Philippi, and finally to Corinth. They washed their tired and calloused feet wherever they found shelter. As was a custom, they washed their clothes with stones and paddles in the public area using *néter* and *borit* as soap and detergent.

Each day found them seeking whatever work they might find, always moving forward, experiencing the heat of the day and the cold of night. When no lodging was available, they slept under the stars. Other times they found the comfort of a lodge, enjoyed a meal with new friends, and listened to the fables and yarns of merchants, sailors, and soldiers.

They did not complain when people cursed or reviled them as foreigners. Prayer, humility, joy, and learning filled their hearts and minds as they traveled the world, growing in the experiences that ordinary men and women lived each day.

Jesus heaved a sigh of relief when they reached the great city of Corinth. Pausing to rest on a bench beneath a sycamore tree, He exhaled with a hearty blow. "From here, My brother, we will go east. Home! Home to our parents and friends. Our venture has been trying at times, but always worth the effort. We traveled far and saw people in the best and worst of times—their love and their rage, their sorrow and their happiness." He smiled, looked down at His tired feet, and took a bite of the apple He had purchased from a farmer. "We worked for some wealthy men, and for those who had little; we saw grown men weep and strong wives carry on when their husbands were ill or dead."

"Indeed," Nur said, smiling to himself as they sat alongside each other, enjoying the sweet crispness of their apples. "I could not count the days and nights we were cold and hungry, but most of the time, we slept on good mats with full bellies, so I have no complaints." He turned to look directly into Jesus' eyes. "Master, we have touched and heard, smelled and tasted the lifestyle of many people." His eyes gleamed as a smile crept across his face. "Nevertheless, I will be glad to go home to our family."

"Then so be it," Jesus replied. "Tomorrow, we strike out for a somewhat roundabout trip home, but first, we must go to Ephesus."

"Why there?"

"When all others have fallen away, you will stand with our mother. You will be her light and strength—her guiding hand. It is you who will lift her to the gates of the Kingdom of God."

"I do not understand, Master."

"No one accepts a prophet in his own land. My mission will not be acceptable to the Nazarenes. When I am gone, My mother will no longer be welcome there. Furthermore, Ephesus will be very special. A few men will become My devoted followers—My apostles. Occasionally, they will need respite from their arduous travels. Ephesus will be near the center of the many lands into which they will travel to deliver My Word. From wherever they are, they can go to My mother's home. In Ephesus, they will find strength, courage, and rest before they once again go among the people of the world with My Father's message.

"Our mother's home," He said wistfully, "will become a kingdom on earth from whence My followers will be renewed in God's love and wisdom." Jesus smiled and rested His hand on Nur's shoulder. "Their work will challenge them physically and spiritually. Under our mother's loving care, and when they have renewed body and soul, the power of the Word will overcome all obstacles, even death itself."

The brothers looked at each other. Their eyes embraced, one to the other. For a moment, time stood still. Once again, the spirit clothed them in an aura of light and wisdom.

"Yes," Nur said. "I will care for our mother and take her where she can live out her life in perpetual adoration, giving praise and glory to You and the Father in heaven while at the same time giving of herself to others."

"So it shall be!" The Messiah looked again into Nur's eyes and repeated Himself. "So it shall be!"

Jesus and Nur experienced pangs of homesickness and the urge to be with their loved ones, but their eagerness to go home made the trip seem even longer. From Corinth, they once again found work on a ship, a large freighter bound for Phoenix on the island of Crete, and from there to Miletus, where they left the ship for the trek to Ephesus.

Though anxious to return to their homeland, they planned to spend enough time in Ephesus to gain knowledge of the area and to prepare an appropriate home for Mary.

Nur did not know when he would return here with Mary, but he wanted to have ample time in the city so that she would have a good home in which to live and serve others.

Jesus suggested they search for a location close to the city yet far enough away to experience the solitude of prayer and contemplation. The home should be sufficient to offer adequate room for Jesus' followers to rest and replenish their vigor for the challenges ahead.

After three days of wandering through the city and its environs, they found a rolling hillside east of Ephesus off the road to Antioch.

Nur beamed when he saw it. Looking up the long road to the house and outbuildings, he thought it to be ideal—a moderate walk into Ephesus, yet far enough away from the city and the highway to fulfill their needs. It stood as an old but solid building perched near the top of the hill with a large, terraced garden sloping down from the house toward the road. A grove of fig trees straddled a crystal-clear trickle of water that flowed from a spring at the rear of the home. A stable and barn were on the side of the hill.

"Surely we have found the right place," Nur exclaimed.

"Yes," Jesus replied. "It seems to be *exactly* what we are seeking."

Easing Himself down on a boulder near the lane to the house, He gave a strong exhale and absorbed the splendor of the land. He smiled, relishing the fragrances of the open countryside.

"I love the thought of her living here," He whispered. "It is perfect."

Nur, too, cast his view to the panoramic, peaceful countryside and imagined what the house would be like in the future. He could re-purpose a room or construct a new building for her oratory. Also, he would inspect all of the rooms to determine if sufficient space existed to lodge the disciples when they came. If not, he would build more rooms. Being more than satisfied with this ideal location, the hard manual labor ahead did not discourage him.

"Indeed," he said aloud, "she is not just our mother, but she will be the spiritual mother to all who follow You." Suddenly he understood the fullness of her role. "From here, she will pour out her love and guidance to all her children. As God is the Father, she is our spiritual mother." He turned to Jesus, who remained seated on the boulder. "Master, at last, I can say I fully comprehend that which will be."

"Come then," Jesus said. "Let us go to the house and talk to the people who live there."

Approaching the front along a pathway that led up from the road, they encountered an elderly man coming out the doorway carrying a tabby cat. Leaning over to put the little feline down by its water dish, he looked up and came face to face with the two strangers.

Jesus spoke. "Good day, sir. I am Jesus of Nazareth." Nodding toward Nur, He introduced him. "Let Me introduce My brother, Nur. And, good sir, who do we have the honor of meeting on this beautiful day?"

The grizzled old man stepped back slightly and gave a noticeable eye to the two men. He neither smiled nor gave any evidence of suspicion, but manifested a degree of concern about speaking to the strangers. "I am Yiorgos. What business do you have with me, sirs?"

Sensing the man's wariness, Jesus responded, "In the next few years, our mother will move away from her homeland—"

The old man interrupted him in midsentence. "If she is happy there, why would she want to move to such a faraway place as Ephesus? What you say sounds nonsensical."

"Life is changing," Jesus said. "Whether slave or freeman, the political and religious atmosphere creates a fragile lifestyle. It is nothing short of tyranny—brother against brother, children against their parents, believers against nonbelievers, and the list goes on."

He looked down when the cat scooted in and cuddled between His feet. He lifted the little ball of fur and held it to His chest while He petted and scratched behind its ears. "If only humans could be as accepting as this cat, life would be filled with love and trust."

Yiorgos chuckled. "Most assuredly, Jesus. So come to the point. What brings you to our home today?"

"We seek to purchase a home for our mother—one close to the city yet far enough away to allow her to enjoy the solitude of the countryside." He gestured to the expanse of open land, looked about, and continued. "Sir, this is exactly what we hope to buy. It is a lovely estate—privacy, a spring with a garden, and what looks like a well-built home."

Yiorgos chuckled again. "I hope it is well built. I did it myself—Lyna, my wife, and I. We built it, but I must say, this is more than coincidence."

"Why is that?" Nur asked.

"Come with me," Yiorgos said while he led them around the house to a bench in the shade beneath a eucalyptus tree. Pouring each of them a cup of water from the spring, he gestured for them to take a seat on the bench. He sat on a stool at the mouth of the spring and leaned forward, resting his elbows on his knees. "Only recently did Lyna and I begin discussing the need to sell this place and move. We're too old to be so far from the shops and our doctor, Rufus—an excellent man who cares for my wife with her female troubles." He paused to give a light chuckle and sip his water before he continued. "So, the gods do hear our prayers, and here you are—two Jews who want to bring their mother to Ephesus."

He smirked, then spoke again. "An old Jew woman in Ephesus, huh? Well, she won't be alone. There are others in the city—businesspeople. Tough as leather, and they have their families, but they don't have much of a synagogue yet. It is little more than an abandoned storehouse. Still, it serves their purpose until they grow their population and can afford to build something more fitting."

Yiorgos shifted around on his rock, adjusted the sash of his tunic, and continued. "Let me tell you, we hoped for a buyer for our property so we could join our daughter and her family in Troas. While not a great distance to travel for you young people, Troas is too far for us to be able to spend time with our daughter and grandchildren. And with my wife's health failing, the house and garden are too much for us to maintain. You are an answer to our wishes. Most people don't want to live this far from the city, and many are too lazy to work the fields, so we are blessed that you came to us."

Jesus turned at the sound of footsteps to see an elderly woman wearing a linen tunic with a shawl around her shoulders coming around the house. She walked with the steady *thunk* of a cane hitting the hard ground, mumbling something unintelligible. When she came closer, she spoke clearly to her husband. "You are as deaf as that stupid cat of yours. You've been talking so loud I could hear from my bed."

Nur stood and gestured for her to take his place on the bench.

Maneuvering carefully with her cane to keep herself steady, she sat next to Jesus and looked directly at Him. "Yes," she said. "You men are an answer to our hopes and dreams. I never thought we would be able to find a buyer. Grace to the gods and thank you for finding us."

The young guests and the elderly couple celebrated the sale of the property with a freshly slaughtered lamb. After dinner, the men sat on stools around a fire, discussing the timing of the transaction. They decided Jesus would travel alone to His parents' home. Nur would remain behind to help the couple sell what they no longer needed and to prepare for the move. After Jesus obtained the money from His family, He would send it via messenger to complete the payment. Then, Yiorgos, Lyna, and Nur would go into

Ephesus to record the sale. From there, Nur would help them make the transition to Troas.

After their discussion, Nur and Jesus retired to the barn to spend the night. As they laid out their mats, Nur looked at Jesus. "What next, Master?" he asked.

"You will prepare this place for our mother and for those who will follow. Do not ask the time, for that is known only to My Father." Jesus put His hands on Nur's arms and spoke softly. "My brother, you will remain here until I send for you. Always be prepared, for you know not when I will call. Until such time, prepare these buildings and pray to our heavenly Father, for great trials and tribulations will follow. People will weep and gnash their teeth. Some will suffer terrible sorrow. Others will gain eternal peace. Many people will disparage the Word of God. Parents will forsake their children. Nations will turn against each other."

Releasing his grip, Jesus stepped back, and each of them retired to their mat.

Lying on his side with His head resting in the crook of His arm, Jesus spoke in a soft, almost melodic tone. "For now, think only of our mother, for she will be known as the mother of the Most High, the Queen of Peace."

Chapter Fifteen
Four Horsemen

Jesus left Ephesus and began His homeward-bound journey, so far away yet so near to the most extraordinary event that would take place in the history of the world. The Son of God would soon begin the work of the one and only God, the King of Kings.

Nur wasted no time in helping the old couple prepare for their move. Walking the streets and alleys, speaking to vendors and shoppers, he found buyers for the household items they no longer needed. By the end of the twenty-seventh day, they had completed all of their business. On the morning of the forty-fourth day, a messenger arrived to deliver the payment for the property. The following day the couple recorded the transaction in the archives of Ephesus, bade farewell to their friends, and began the trek to Troas with Nur serving as their guide.

He returned to his *new* home near Ephesus on the sixty-fifth day after Jesus had departed. That night after offering prayers, he washed his hands, ate a portion of bread he had purchased in the city, and finished his simple meal with a bunch of grapes from the vineyard. After dining and on the verge of physical exhaustion, he laid out his mat and slept.

The soft, gentle coo of a mourning dove roused him at daybreak. Slipping on his sandals and wrapping a woolen tunic over his shoulders, he went to the spring for water, then to the top of the hill where he fell to his knees in prayer.

"Abba," he prayed, "I shall follow Your voice through the passage of eternity. Lead me where You will. Speak to me that which You will. Command me as You will. Your Son, Jesus, is the Savior of the World. I thank You for the mission upon which I have embarked and seek Your hand to guide me through each day's journey. I pray this until the end of time when I will join You and the angels and saints of Your kingdom."

Prostrating himself on the hard, stony ground, he continued. "I will begin this day by surveying everything—the grounds, the house, and the stable. I will learn of all that is here and is useful, and I will prepare all that is necessary for the mother of the Messiah and His followers. When the time comes, each of them will find warmth and comfort. This place will become a pleasant repose for all who enter."

He rose to his knees and lifted his arms to the heavens as the morning sun bathed his face. "My God, my God," he said aloud, "unto You, I give all that I may. For You, I go about this day's work that it will stand as a monument to Your goodness and glory forever and ever, amen."

Nur labored for more than a year, cleaning out decades of wear and grime that had accumulated on the interior and exterior of the solidly built house. It was adequate for three or four people but would be too small to ensure the comfort of Mary and those who would follow the Master.

He had surveyed the property and laid out a grid for the new rooms he would build. He would begin by adding two rooms for sleep, a large common room for prayer and meals, and a small house to serve as the oratory for the mother of the Son of God.

To accommodate the preparation of meals, he would construct a work area with a fireplace and a *tannur* oven in a shaded space between the buildings.

Nur had been a well-trained student from the master teacher of carpentry and masonry—Joseph. Having learned his skills from the ultimate instructor, Nur's trained eyes missed nothing. He joyfully accepted the tasks of rebuilding the shelves, scrubbing down the walls, refurbishing the tables and closets, restoring timbers and rails on the roof, and repairing some of the well-worn path from the highway.

He labored from early light to darkness every day except the Sabbath. He observed the Sabbath from sunset on the sixth day and continued the prescribed rituals until he observed the three stars in the night sky on the seventh day. He rose early on the Sabbath, attended the synagogue in Ephesus, and spent the day fasting and praying, asking God for strength and guidance, and offering thanks for the blessings of the previous week.

On the night of the three stars, he ate a meal of cheese and two small loaves of bread with water to drink. Then he would sleep restfully, ready to begin the work of God the following morning.

At the end of the first year and carrying a skin of wine, he climbed a distant hilltop where he looked down with an overview of his handiwork. Finding a shady spot beneath an elm tree, he sat down and enjoyed a sip of sweet wine. He gazed across the lowlands that separated him from Mary's house while a gentle breeze dried the sweat from his brow. Satisfied, and knowing Joseph would be proud of his work, he realized the efforts bore the mark of one of the finest craftsmen in the land—not him, but the always meticulous and patient Joseph. Not only would the home in Ephesus serve Mary's needs, but it would provide the elegance she merited.

Another week passed. At midmorning, Nur was working in the fields, cleaning weeds from the trickle of water that fed the fig trees. He heard horses' hooves pounding on the highway from Ephesus. He could see nothing over the low-lying hills, but the sounds grew closer and closer. Laying the hoe on the ground and walking up the hillside toward the house, he associated the sound of horses with Roman soldiers. No good could come from that. His heart pounded at the thought. Throwing aside the waterskin he carried over his shoulder, he ran the remaining few steps to the front door.

In the distance, four riders and a team of white horses pulling a cart turned off the highway between Antioch and Ephesus and continued up the lane toward him. He had never anticipated the thought of Romans with their nonbelievers' hearts and minds coming to this hillside redoubt dedicated to the work of the Messiah. It could not bode well.

Chapter Sixteen
Petropoulos

Nur stood resolutely in the doorway and prayed, "Glorious God, help me to protect this temporal foundation for the work of Your Son, Jesus." He wiped the sweat from his brow and spoke aloud, struggling to assure himself he could dissuade them from destroying this holy site. "Lord God, with Your guiding hand, these people will come in peace, not to destroy this source of salvation."

The riders continued their steady pace, coming closer with every heartbeat. When they were less than a quarter-league away, Nur saw they were not soldiers. A woman was the single occupant of a cart. She held the reins in one hand and a whip in the other. He had never seen anything like this—a woman driving her cart pulled by a magnificent team of white horses. It was a sight to behold.

It was not only a woman, but four male riders close behind her and two pack animals following the last rider. Nur's mind scrambled. *If not Romans, then who? Greeks! But who would be coming here? What business would any Greek have with us? Surely they must be lost and in need of direction.*

Hurrying into the house, he snatched up a jug to fill with fresh water from the spring. Running to the source of cool water, he glanced over his shoulder. The team and riders pulled up the hill. They raced past the fig trees and up the final leg of the lane to the house. A billowing dust cloud enveloped them.

Nur hurried to the top of the lane where it ended near the house. He choked when the cloud of dust rolled over him and clogged his nostrils.

Soaked in lather and dripping with sweat, the horses flared their nostrils with each breath.

The woman spoke first. "Sir!" she said respectfully when she looked at Nur. "We seek Jesus, the Nazarene. Do you know him?"

The tallest and the eldest of the men slipped down from his horse, holding its reins and striding forward to take the team's reins from the woman.

"Thank you, Alexandros," she said as she stepped down from her cart.

Nur stood motionless in the doorway, unsure how to answer.

"You must be his brother, Nur," she commented when she stepped toward him. "I know you are not Jesus because of your blue eyes." Her face wrinkled with frustration as she spoke. "Well?"

"Yes, my lady. I am Nur, His brother, but He is not here." Nur moved aside and gestured into the house. "Will you and the men come in?"

She nodded acquiescence, then followed Nur into the house. "Thank you for your hospitality. Will you show my sons where they can stable the animals while I refresh myself?"

Nur gave her a clean cloth and jug of water, then showed her to a room where she could wash the grit of the road from her body. When he went outside again, the men had removed the saddles and bridles. In a few minutes, they brushed the horses and led them into the stable, where they found water and grain. The youngest of the men carried the packs from the horses and flopped them on the ground by the door. The others stepped past him and went inside to drink and refresh themselves.

Coming from the back room, the woman held the cloth in her hand, delicately dabbing the water from her brow as she spoke. "My name is Athena, the wife of Petropoulos, whom I believe you know."

"Indeed, my lady," Nur replied. "But what brings you here, and how did you know where to find us?"

"You and your brother sailed only one voyage with my husband, but he never stopped talking about you." She sat on a straw-filled pallet and leaned against the wall while she brushed back her scarf. Her dark hair was wet with sweat. She paused for a moment as she gently wiped it with the cloth. "That is," she said, "he never stopped talking about you until his death."

"His death?" Nur blurted. "What happened? How did he die?" He quickly crossed the room and sat on a pallet beside her. The four men found seats on a bench where they shared a jug of water and a loaf of bread Nur gave them.

"They were unloading bags of grain off his ship," she said. "It was just a simple accident, but a rope slipped, and the bales fell on him." She paused for a moment, composing herself, then continued. "The bales broke almost every bone in his body. His crew brought him home to die. No physician could help him, he was hurt so badly."

She held the cloth in her hands, wringing it ever so tightly. Tears filled her eyes when she spoke. "On his deathbed, he spoke of Jesus and you. He spoke of the chill in his blood when Jesus talked to him. He often mentioned there was some deep, dark secret about the two of you."

She looked directly into Nur's eyes. "At first, Jesus frightened him, but after you and Jesus departed, my husband sensed he understood the truth. Candidly, he never liked or believed in our gods, yet knew nothing else. That's when the two of you entered his life. When Jesus spoke of heaven, my husband realized your belief in the afterlife is not so different from what we believe. There is the passage from this world to the other, the joy of paradise by whatever name it is known. But, if that is true and our brass or golden gods are not true gods, then your God must be the one true God."

She smiled as she continued her lecture, as if convincing herself of what she was saying. "If goldsmiths or glaziers can make our gods with their hands, how can those products of man be God? The answer is obvious. Those material objects are not gods. They are just statues and ornaments, nothing more.

"On his deathbed, my husband commanded us to sell all we had and to search until we found you." She glanced at her sons, then looked directly into Nur's eyes, took his hands into her own, and continued. "Show us how we may be with Jesus and learn of the true God." She got up, stepped across the room, and stood beside her sons. "These young men and I will stay and serve. All we ask is that we know the truth of the one real God—that we know of your kingdom in heaven. We seek no more than that."

"So it shall be," replied Nur. Rising, he extended his hand in friendship to the four young men.

Athena introduced her sons to him. Didymus, the youngest, looked about fourteen. Much shorter than his brothers, he gave away nothing to them in stature—broad shoulders, trim hips, and powerfully built legs.

Johannes, the next youngest, stood beside Didymus. Half a head taller than his younger brother, Johannes was sleek of build but showed trim, strong muscles in his arms and legs.

Philip, the third brother, stood nearly as tall as his older brother. Philip's skin was the darkest of the four, and his curly black hair reminded Nur of Jesus. While not appearing as strong as his older brother, Philip smiled little but silently observed. Listening, not speaking, was his most notable characteristic, Nur would discover.

Alexandros was clearly the new patriarch of the family. His muscular body alone was intimidating enough to pronounce him a leader. He was quick of wit with polite discourse and was protective of his mother.

Nur made casual note of each of their characteristics. Alexandros, by age and size, was the leader. Philip was the most contemplative. Johannes easily bridged the age difference between the older and the younger brothers, being careful not to favor one over the others. Didymus was a more youthful brother who had to put up with the *guidance* of his older brothers.

"Nur," said Alexandros, "we promised our father to find you and Jesus, so we have carried out the first portion of our debt to him. Nevertheless, we have much more to do to fulfill our promise."

"My friend," interjected Philip as he straightened his back and stood tall, "we remain true to our father. We devote our lives—each of us. We dedicate our lives to learning about the true God. To that end, even if we must spend our entire lives, so be it. We will do whatever you and Jesus call upon us to do. Our father was a wise man, and when he spoke of your God and the place you call heaven, then we believed. This was not an easy decision. We thought our father was delirious with pain when he spoke about you. When we discussed it among ourselves, we concluded this was his final gift to us—the gift of a true God. For that, we will always be grateful."

Athena and her sons worked with Nur throughout the summer and fall to the onset of winter. Under his guidance, they built another house near the trees at the foot of the hill. Here, the sons of Petropoulos would live, serving as gatekeepers at the home of Mary and the followers of Jesus. At the main house, the men subdivided the main room for Athena, where she would have privacy and a place to sleep. Also, here she would be close to Mary and the followers so she could contribute to their assistance whenever needed.

Nur and the four brothers worked from dawn until midday each day, but when the sun reached its peak, they stopped to eat the meal Athena had prepared. After eating, they adjourned to mats on the floor and sat around Nur, who spoke to them of the prophets and other great patriarchs—of Noah and Isaac, of Moses, Abraham, Jacob, and David. They spoke of God's promise to send a Savior to free mankind and to show them the way to eternal salvation. A God invisible to the eye, but a God of faith and trust, love and forgiveness, a God who promised everlasting life in His heavenly kingdom.

Many months passed. Nur shared the love of God and His promises to mankind, but one secret he kept to himself—the secret of Jesus, the Messiah. By winter, they had nearly completed their work. Nur and Didymus hung the door to Athena's room just in time. Dark storm clouds rolled across the valley and swept up the hill toward the house.

Each of the men packed away their tools and took shelter in the main room, even though it was only late morning, too early to eat their midday meal. They laughed at themselves, soaked to the bone, water dripping from their clothes onto the floor.

Suddenly, and with no fanfare, Athena entered the room. Her face was ashen. Beads of perspiration dotted her forehead. Her hands and lips trembled when she tried to speak. Though her mouth was as dry as the desert floor and her lips parched as dried clay, she spoke. "He has come to me."

"What are you saying?" Philip asked as he and Alexandros helped her take a seat on a cushion.

Glancing from one son to another, she forced the slightest hint of a smile. "He came to me. It was a bright light, so bright I could not see." She paused to look at Nur. "I was about to prepare the meal. Suddenly, there was a dazzling light—brighter than the sun. It was…" She paused, dabbing tears that streamed from her eyes, then continued. "It was so bright I thought I was dead. But instantly, I knew the truth. It was not my death, but my rebirth."

She glanced again at each of her sons. Her voice was soft and motherly. "He spoke to me. I heard His voice and felt His love. Your God is my God." She reached out her arms to her children. One by one, they came to her, and she embraced them.

Nur stood nearby, watching until she spoke to him.

"Now is the time that you must go to your brother. Come to me, my child." She held her arms out to Nur. He crouched down beside her, and she held him close. "The Lord God told me you must return without delay. Your family needs you now. You must not stay here any longer. We will keep the house and fields for your return, whenever that may be."

"Did you see Him, Mother?" Didymus inquired.

"No, my child. His brightness is too great for us, as mortal beings, to see. But He spoke to me, and I felt His presence. The Lord God of Israel is the one true God. Let us never question that so long as we live, even though we shall never see Him until we reside in paradise." She gazed with a mother's love at Nur. "My blessed son, prepare to leave us. Carry only what you need, but nothing else. I will load a bag with bread and fruit."

Glancing at Johannes, she spoke. "Fill two skins with fresh water. Help him prepare, for he must not stay in this house tonight."

Chapter Seventeen
Joseph

Unable to travel by sea due to the various ships' schedules, Nur set out overland. The days became a blur, one blending into the other. He journeyed over the highlands and deserts of Galatia, across the lowlands, and on toward Tarsus. Alone and on foot, he followed the narrow highway to Antioch and southward along the shores of the Great Sea. He spent minimal time eating and sleeping, always anxious to answer the Master's call. The cold winter served him well because the dry summer heat would sap his strength. Now, though, he stopped only on the Sabbath to rest and pray in the synagogue.

Still two days' journey from home, a mongrel dog took up with him on the road. With no extra food or drink, Nur struggled to no avail to shoo off the skinny, floppy-eared mutt. "Can't you see, you ugly little thing, I have nothing to offer you? Go," he snapped with a flick of his wrist.

The mongrel looked at him with pleading eyes, then lay down and rolled over.

Nur curled his lip. As a Judean, dogs were considered unclean and seldom kept as pets. However, his Egyptian experience from many years ago taught him that if dogs had been trained correctly, they could be pleasant family pets and watchdogs.

Nur chuckled in self-deprecation at his inner turmoil. "Dog," he muttered when he squatted down and rubbed the mutt's belly, "you should be a teacher because you certainly have a way of expressing yourself."

Reaching into his bag, he took a small chunk of bread and offered it to his newly found pet. Without hesitation, the dog snatched it away and swallowed it in one gulp.

Rising to his feet, Nur looked at the dog and conceded, "Okay, come with me, but the trip may be more arduous than you think." Continuing down the road, Nur looked down at the dog and commented, "I cannot simply call you 'dog.' You must have a name, so I have one that is very fitting for you. I shall call you Ontos, which means 'thing' in Greek. I will name you that because I have no idea what kind of dog you are or where you came from." He chuckled as he patted his leg and called his new friend to follow him. "Come, Ontos, let's go home."

The last rays of sunlight eased over the horizon. But finally, after weeks of journeying, Nur reached the foot of the path that led to the home of Jesus, Mary, and Joseph. He sat on the ground with his feet in a shallow ditch at the entrance to the trail.

Ontos eased himself into the ditch, spun himself in little circles padding down the dirt, then curled up at Nur's feet.

Doves swooped in their evening flight pattern toward the spring at the side of the house. Somewhere in the distance, a dog bayed mournfully. Ontos sat upright and twisted his head to listen.

The distant yapping did not disturb Nur. He rested quietly, absorbing the blissful solitude of the fading sunlight. His journey was over. Ahead lay the work of the Master. He lingered for a few more minutes, bathing in the serenity emanating from his adopted parents' home.

A flicker of light from the window penetrated the gathering darkness. Mary appeared in the doorway, carrying a lamp to the table a few steps away from the door.

He took a deep breath. It had been so long since he feasted on the celestial beauty of the mother of the Messiah. Shifting his weight, he accidentally stepped on Ontos' toes. The dog jumped and gave a quick, sharp yap that pierced the peace of the sunset.

Mary glanced in Nur's direction.

Goosebumps crawled over his arms and legs. Their eyes met. "Mother!" he cried.

Mary ran down the path toward him, calling out, "My child, my blessed child!" They met halfway down the path. She wrapped her arms around him, held him tightly, and whispered into his ear, "God has blessed us this day." Her tears streamed down his and her cheeks as she sobbed in joy. She breathed deeply and hugged him even more tightly.

Nur was breathless and unable to speak. The power of her love overwhelmed him. Though exhausted from his journey, newly found energy pulsed through his veins.

Grasping his shoulders, Mary stepped back to look at him at arm's length. Her lips curled into a motherly smile when she saw his tired face and dirty clothes. "Look at you," she said, hugging him again and kissing his cheek. "My child, my child, how I have missed you." She stepped slowly away from him, holding his hand in hers as she led him up the path to their home. Turning her gaze to the mongrel at her feet, she looked back at Nur. "Is there an explanation for this?"

Nur shrugged his shoulders and gave a cheerful smirk. "He keeps me company."

"Then he, too, is home," she replied as she reached down and patted the dog's scruffy ears, then continued toward the house.

Ontos followed behind and wagged his tail, sensing a meal and sleep.

Mary picked up the lantern as they passed by the table and held it high so they could see. "Jesus told me you were coming, so every night I placed a lantern on the table as a guide to beckon you home." She stopped abruptly when they reached the doorway and spoke in a soft, gentle tone. "Before we go further, there is something I must tell you." Tears welled in her eyes. Her voice quaked as she spoke. "Joseph, my husband and your father, is dead."

Nur stiffened. A cold chill ran through his body. Turning at the sound of footsteps coming from the house, he came face-to-face with Jesus—His face somber yet filled with peace and kindness. "Nur," He murmured as they embraced. "Welcome home, My brother. Welcome home."

Mary dabbed her eyes with the cuff of her sleeve, then excused herself and went to prepare their evening meal.

Nur watched her walk into the house before he spoke. "Tell me about our father," he implored. "I had no idea he had become ill, or I would have hurried even more. I'm sorry I was not here when I should have been."

"No, no. Don't concern yourself," Jesus replied. "You could not have helped him; the time had come. He had fulfilled the duties placed upon him by the Lord our God. It was proper when he left the bounds of earth as his wife and I stood by his bedside. He was at peace and in the arms of God Almighty."

Jesus gazed upon Nur, and once again the spirit passed between them. With His arm over His brother's shoulder, they went inside where they sat at the table.

Jesus continued. "Truly, My brother, I miss him so much. His kind and good words. His advice. I miss his hands guiding Me as I try to make a straight cut on a piece of timber. His advice will always ring true in My mind: 'Measure twice, but cut once.'"

They had heard Joseph's advice so many times they couldn't stop themselves from laughing.

"I miss everything about him," Jesus said, "but the time had come. His work on earth had been completed. God provided him a compassionate death of joy and wisdom, not one of illness or pain. He died a most blessed person and lives this very moment with the Lord God."

Jesus sat quietly and looked through the window and into the growing darkness of the night sky. Somewhere in the distance, a dog continued its mournful howl. The stars glowed in the eastern sky and peace settled over the countryside.

Nur broke the silence. "Now, my brother?"

Jesus rose and walked several steps, then turned and looked back at Nur. "The time has come for Me to go about My Father's bidding. We have always talked about tomorrow, but tomorrow has come. I love you, Nur. As I go about that which I must do, I call upon you to care for our mother. She is strong and loving, but she misses her husband's companionship. She cries in loneliness, yet her heart is filled with joy."

Jesus paced back and forth, then turned to Nur.

"As My mission arrives, so does yours. Care for her forever, for this is the command of God."

"As You accept Your mission, I assume mine with humble gratitude," Nur replied.

Mary stepped from the doorway as her sons grasped each other's hands. A warm glow settled over the three of them, an aura of the colors of the rainbow surrounded them, and a sweet, pleasant scent swept over the landscape. They held each other for a few moments, and Mary observed again the extraordinary grace that flowed between her children. She was pleased.

The following week, Mary and her sons journeyed to Cana for the marriage of Ruth, the daughter of Rachel and Nadab. She had been betrothed to Abram, the son of Joseph of Arimathea, a member of the Sanhedrin. The newly wedded couple were grateful for the many friends who traveled long distances to share their happy and holy ceremony.

The marriage feast had not yet neared completion when Mary noticed many guests had yet to eat and drink their fill. While there was ample food, she noticed that nearly all the wine had been drunk. She knew the bride and groom would be embarrassed if the beverages were consumed before the guests could finish their food and drinks.

Nur sat at her side while Jesus conversed with friends whom He had not seen in many months. Mary leaned over and whispered to Nur, "Tell the servants to come to me but tell them to do so without fanfare. I must speak to them immediately."

Nur looked at his mother, who pointed at two servants seated in the shade. "Yes, Mother." Approaching the servants, he spoke softly and nodded toward Mary. "My friends, the lady seeks your service, but be about it quietly."

They caught her glance and walked around the crowd to approach her. "Yes, my lady," said the elder of the two.

Mary glanced in the direction of the nearly empty wine jugs. "The wine is nearly gone. Do you have more?"

"No, my lady," replied the first.

"Then do as I say." She gestured in the direction of her son. "Go to the tall man there. He is my Son. Tell Him I sent you, then do as He says."

With that command, the servants went to Him. "Sir, your mother said we should speak to You. What is it You command?"

Jesus, Andrew, Simon Peter, and three other men were in conversation when the servant approached Him. Hearing the servant's comments, He stepped away from his friends and walked through the crowd to His mother.

"The wine," she said when she glanced at the jugs.

"What business is that of mine? I'm not responsible for the refreshments," He replied.

"As Your mother and speaking for Your dear friends, please, Jesus, now is the time to begin that which you must accomplish, and it is here where it must begin."

Jesus said nothing but looked into her eyes, then kissed her cheek and replied, "So it shall be." He turned to the servants. "Go to the well and fill the jugs. Bring them here so I may taste the water. Be hasty, for your master's guests are in need."

Having filled the jugs, the servants brought them to Jesus and aligned them before Him. Jesus stepped forward and, with a small cup, tasted a few drops from each jug. When He finished, He turned to the servants and commanded them to serve the wine to the guests.

"But, Master—" one began.

The second servant interrupted, "Master, what have you done?"

"Go now," Jesus commanded. "Say nothing to anyone. Serve the wine. There is plenty for all of them, and they can eat and drink to their contentment."

On the journey home, Jesus went only as far as Nazareth, then bade Mary and Nur goodbye. "I go now to the synagogue to pray, but you must continue home."

"Where will you go?" Mary asked. "What can we do for you?"

Jesus took His mother in His arms and held her tightly.

Nur stood nearby, embarrassed and unsure of what he should do while the Messiah clung to His mother.

Finally, Jesus released her and looked at Nur. "Brother, behold your mother." He turned and looked at Mary. She wept quietly. Speaking softly and with a slight nod toward Nur, He said, "Mother, behold your son."

Jesus' face filled with a gentle kindness as he spoke His last words before embarking upon His Father's mission.

"Honor the Lord, our God, with all your heart and with all of your soul; honor Him with your work and prayers; honor Him with all you do, and with all you refuse to do. May His way guide your every breath, for your reward resides in the Kingdom of Heaven."

Nur held Mary's hand as Jesus turned and walked down the side street toward the synagogue. Nur examined every detail as He strode away: His long, measured stride; the robe thrown over His shoulder nearly dragging the ground; an old but comfortable pair of sandals protecting His feet; His long, dark hair and beard; His face set like flint, but filled with love and compassion: a man, yet the child of God.

The thought sent chills through Nur's body. The Son of God was going to the synagogue from this nondescript intersection where two insignificant streets met. From there, He would continue to Capernaum and elsewhere—to the mountains and the deserts and beyond the seas. He would preach to Jews and gentiles, and lead men and women of all races to the truth of God, not as men would have it be, but as it truly always had been, was, and would be forever: a truth untarnished by men's ways, unblemished by powerful men's rules and desires, a truth as straightforward as love and forgiveness. A truth so simple and easy to grasp yet so complex and difficult to hold.

"Come, Mother," Nur said when Jesus disappeared from their view. "Let us go home and offer prayers for Him. Then let us eat a meal and rest, for as His work is underway, so too is ours. We must pray daily and often for Him and His followers."

"Tell me, Nur," said Mary as they walked from the city and toward Nain, "what else do you know? What has Jesus told you?"

They walked some distance while Nur considered his response. "We know neither the hour nor the day upon which we may be called, but we must always be prepared."

They walked on, the chilly night air causing them to wrap their cloaks tightly around their shoulders. They were nearly home before Nur continued.

"Some will heed Him. Some will reject Him. Nevertheless, people will hear of His work throughout the world, even in places unknown to our scholars. He mentioned a place called Bac that is far away—a place where waters gather. Jesus' followers will take His Word and give it to people who yearn for the truth."

Nur put his arm around Mary's shoulders and held her close for the duration of the walk home.

As they approached the gate, he offered one last comment. "Those in authority will reject your child. Their power and fear of the truth will pierce your heart, and I will take you from this land at that time. We will travel to your new home near Ephesus. From there, you will provide guidance and love, and even a little food and water and fresh goat's milk for Jesus' disciples. As surely as Jesus is the Son of God, you shall be known as the Spiritual Mother of His church."

He paused and looked into her eyes.

"I will stand alongside you forever."

Chapter Eighteen
Until Jerusalem

The seasons rolled by—winter into spring and spring into summer. As fall approached, Nur set out for Ephesus to visit and pray with Athena and her sons. It was pleasing for him to find that the young men, especially Didymus, had honed their skills with their brains and brawn.

Using only the most basic of tools, Didymus had gone through the interior and exterior of the original house, chipping away the old chinking from between the timbers and rocks. Using a mixture of sand, ground stone dust, and water, he mixed a newer and stronger chinking—strong enough to last many years. His skill and materials were sufficient to maintain the warmth of the fire inside and ward off the cold winter air from penetrating the walls.

Philip, too, had excelled. He memorized Nur's preaching and, in turn, taught daily lessons to his mother and brothers. He mastered the stories of the prophets and of the kingdom of God, reflecting on the values of the great peoples of history.

With Athena as the matriarch, Alexandros assumed the role of a good and loving head of the household.

Johannes developed his skill at bartering for labor, which he and his brothers would provide in exchange for goods or money. Didymus became the primary worker, maintaining the buildings and fields and tending the animals.

They worked in harmony, satisfied that they would see the one true God one day.

Nur spent several weeks with them, strengthening their faith in God and teaching them the love and honor they would find in the service of the King of Kings. As the depth of wintertime passed and the first signs of spring broke free, he again set out for Nazareth and Nain. He would not see Athena and her sons again until the Son of Man had risen from the dead.

At the beginning of the second winter came the first opportunity for Jesus and Nur to see each other since the wedding at Cana, although Jesus had visited Mary a few days while Nur was in Ephesus.

The sun had long set over the horizon, and a hazy sky blanketed the valley. Nur built a fire, and he and Mary offered prayers of thanksgiving and finished their evening meal. Ontos lay beneath the table and waited for a few scraps of food. With a soft heart for the tired, old dog, Mary tore off a tidbit of bread and leaned down to feed him. He snatched it out of her hand and swallowed it in one gulp. Pausing momentarily, Ontos raised his head slightly, cocked his ears, and listened. With a soft growl, he rose and faced the doorway.

"Is someone coming?" Mary asked.

Nur rose from his cushion and stepped toward the door. "Shhh," he commanded as Ontos crept alongside him, still giving a deep-throated growl. Taking a lamp in his hand, Nur opened the door and stepped outside. Hearing footsteps approaching the house, he called out, "Who comes?"

"It is I," came the response.

Jesus was home!

Mary ran to the open door as the Son of God reached the doorway. She grabbed Him around His neck and kissed His cheeks while He grasped her around the waist. Leaning back and safe in her Son's arms, Mary admired Him from head to toe. "Jesus, Jesus," she exclaimed. "We have missed you so much." Stepping free from His strong hands, she gestured to the dinner table as Nur cleared it and made way for Jesus to be seated. "We have smoked Comb fish and fresh bread," she said while she scooted a cushion into place for Him to sit.

"And figs I picked today from the orchard—sweet and juicy," Nur said.

Mary gave a soft chuckle. "We must not forget the cheese. I bought it at the marketplace this morning."

Jesus kicked off His sandals and lowered Himself comfortably on the cushion.

Mary laid out the meal while He drank from a cup of wine.

Jesus paused and looked lovingly at her, then at the food she had prepared. "Sit with me," He said as His eyes passed from Mary to Nur. "Let us pray."

With His mother seated to one side and His brother at the other, He took their hands in His.

Lifting His eyes to heaven, He prayed, "My heavenly Father, we offer our gratitude for the feast set on this humble table. To You, we offer every moment of our lives in thanksgiving for the limitless gifts and mercy You bestow upon us. Strengthen us for what lies ahead, for the way is narrow and steep. Still, with Your endless love and strength, we will undertake all that is necessary to spread Your love, mercy, and eternal love throughout the world."

Completing His prayer, Jesus consumed the meal His mother and brother had set before Him. He paused only once to slip a piece of bread to the ever-vigilant dog whose eyes never left the Master.

Afterward, Jesus stretched out on a mat. "Mother," He said, grinning, "no one else can fix such a splendid meal." He glanced at Nur, still seated at the table. "My brother, how are you not the size of a wine pot?"

The two brothers and their mother enjoyed a good laugh that roused Ontos from a nap where he had curled up close to Nur's feet.

Jesus looked down at him, then patted His own leg. "Come here, My scraggly friend."

The dog hesitated, looked up at Nur, then jumped up and ran to Jesus. The Master patted his floppy ears, and Ontos rolled over and allowed Jesus to scratch his belly.

Jesus snickered. "I know it sounds trite, but there is no finer place than home, no finer time than a good meal and the love of one's family." He chuckled at Ontos and again scratched the dog's floppy ears. "And a good dog."

Jesus spent a week with His family but spoke little of His travels. He worked the sheep with Nur, helped clean out the stables, then assumed the dirty burden of cleaning weeds from the dribble of water that flowed from the spring to the trees.

Mary preferred Jesus to rest for the short time He would be home, enjoy some free time, and eat to His heart's content. It surprised Nur to hear her speak so strongly to Him, telling him to take more time and effort to care for Himself. As His mother, she knew what He needed. "Nur can manage the tasks around the house. But it would help if You rested," she commanded.

"Mother, hear my words." Jesus' voice and expression were filled with compassion. "There is little time before the reign of God is at hand. Let Me be about that which I must and work with Nur. I will have ample time to rest, but for now, let Me find pleasure where I may."

Mary accepted His gentle rebuke with a smile, then spoke in her motherly manner. "It is as You command. I ask only that You give up the work during the heat of the day and come and pray with me."

He smiled and nodded. "So it shall be. Each day through the afternoon's heat, we shall pray for the Lord's blessings on all His children."

Jesus returned home once during the passing of each of the seasons but stayed no more than three or four days. He slept until dawn, worked with Nur, prayed with His mother, and enjoyed the evening meal with Ontos alert for an errant bit of food.

Near the end of his mission's third winter, Jesus spoke of the upcoming Passover. He took Mary's hands in his own. "Come with Nur to Jerusalem for the Passover. We shall break bread with our friends—Peter, Andrew, James, and My strongest followers. We will gather those who have heard the Word of God, and together we shall give thanks. The peace of the Lord is upon us now and forever." He kissed Mary and Nur, then opened the door to leave. He paused to pet Ontos, then spoke gently, "Until Jerusalem."

Chapter Nineteen
Passover

A messenger came to Mary and Nur, telling them to meet Jesus in Bethany, where they would meet with His friends, Mary of Magdala, her sister Martha, and Lazarus.

Nur loaded a pack on a donkey and prepared a second animal for Mary to ride. Because of traditional enmity with the Samaritans, Nur mapped a route eastward toward Scythopolis, then south along the river toward Jericho, and onto the trip's final leg to Bethany. The detour took an extra day, so they arrived in Bethany late in the afternoon of the fourth day, only a short time after Jesus and His followers had arrived.

Martha and Mary prepared a meal in Bethany for Jesus and His family. Before the Master took a seat at the place of honor, the two sisters called Him aside. They placed a cushion on the floor, and at their request, He sat down. Martha removed His sandals and took the ointment of spikenard perfume from Mary.

Martha spoke softly and tenderly as she dripped the expensive perfume on His feet. "Master, allow me, a faithful servant, to cleanse Your feet." She looked into His eyes and continued. "You have traveled so far and done so much in the name of Your Father. I am honored to be in Your presence and to refresh Your tired feet."

Jesus looked deeply into her eyes. His voice was soft and tender. "Martha, few people will understand the truth you hold in your soul. I accept the honor you bestow upon me." Reaching out and touching her hands, He continued, "Your strength will carry you through many hardships yet to come. Despite those things, you will be safeguarded from the evildoers and reside forever in the heavenly kingdom of My Father."

Using the sash of her gown, she bathed His feet and dried them with her hair.

One of His followers, Judas Iscariot, rebuked Him, saying, "Why have you allowed this to happen? We could have sold that ointment and used the money to feed the poor."

Without comment, Jesus eyed Judas, then nodded to the sisters to prepare a place for Him at the table. Rising from the cushion, He turned to Judas and spoke tenderly, "Leave her alone. Let her keep it for the day they prepare for my burial. The poor you will always have, but me you will not always have."

The following day, Nur prepared a donkey for Mary to ride into the city. When he began to prepare a second donkey for the Messiah, Jesus interrupted him. "Stop, Nur." Turning his attention to Philip and James, He commanded them, "Go into the city. There you will find a young foal tied to a tree. Untie it and bring it to me."

"Master," Philip said, "what about the owner?"

"Tell him the Master has need for it, then carry out My instructions."

As He directed, the two men departed into Jerusalem to fetch the foal as Jesus had told them to do.

The mother of the Messiah rode astride a donkey while Nur led them into the city.

Shortly after that, James and Philip returned, leading the foal. They immediately placed a blanket on its back and turned to Jesus. Without hesitation, He hoisted Himself upon the young animal and began His way into the city.

Jerusalem and the roads leading into it overflowed with men, women, and children during Passover. Still, today they were even more crowded because so many people had heard of Jesus of Nazareth. They sought Him, hoping to witness His miracles. Some prayed for a cure for themselves or a family member; others wanted at least to lay their eyes upon Him.

Nur listened intently when he and Mary passed through the crowds along the roadway. He smiled, satisfied that so many Jews and even some Greeks proclaimed Jesus the Messiah. Indeed, this Passover would mark an exceptional fulfillment to the honor and glory of the living God.

As they approached the city's gates, Mary commanded Nur to halt. She wished to wait in the shade of a tree. From there, she would witness the entry of her Son, the Messiah, into the holy city. Nur removed the sheepskin blanket from the donkey's back, arranged it on the ground for her to rest on, and then fetched a jug of water. An hour passed before Nur heard a clamor of people shouting and throwing palm branches on the road for Jesus to ride over.

"Hosanna," they shouted over and over. "Hosanna! Blessed is He who comes in the name of the Lord! Blessed is the King of the Jews!"

Jesus looked upon His mother and brother with compassion as He passed by them astride the young foal. Then, Nur recalled the Scripture: *"Fear not, O daughter of Zion! Your king approaches you on a donkey's colt."*

Jesus, His mother, brother, and friends Lazarus, Martha, Mary, and the other disciples went to the home of a man whose name Nur did not know. Jesus had directed them to follow a manservant carrying a water jug, a man they would encounter when they entered the city. The entourage followed him through the streets and came to a large but modest home near the city's center. James, one of the disciples, spoke to the servant when he approached the gate to the house.

Nur stood by Mary, who sat at ease on the donkey, and they watched the servant converse with James. The servant excused himself and dashed through the gate and into the house. While they awaited his return, Jesus came to His mother and helped her to dismount. They spoke softly for a moment, and when they moved toward the gate, the homeowner, his wife, several children, and two servants approached them.

"Blessed is my family," the man cried out. "Welcome to our home." He opened the gate and fell to his knees, welcoming Jesus and His followers to celebrate the Passover in his home.

The man's name was Nicolas, and his wife was Abiah. Their oldest son, who was nine years old, was Mathan, and the next oldest child, about seven years old, was Jacob. The youngest was a girl of two or three years named Naomi. They were a devout Jewish family, serving the temple, feeding and clothing the poor, yet prosperous and fair in the marketplace.

Nicolas had been in Bethany when Jesus raised Lazarus from the dead. When Nicolas returned home, he had proclaimed to his family, "I have seen with mine own eyes Jesus of Nazareth. This man is more than a great prophet, for I have witnessed along with many others. He is the Messiah. Blessed are we that He has come. Praise be to Israel."

Nicolas led Jesus, His family, and His followers to an upper room, barren except for two tables and some benches. Abiah brought mats upstairs for the visitors to rest on while she and the other women prepared the Passover meal. The children carried water jugs and clean towels for the guests to wash themselves and drink the fresh water the servant had delivered.

When evening approached, Peter and James pushed the tables together, forming a long rectangular place where Jesus and His followers could sit comfortably. When the tables were in place, the children arranged benches so everyone could hear and see the Master when He spoke.

With the preparations complete, Abiah approached Jesus. "Master, the Passover meal is ready to be served. Will You take the seat of honor?"

Jesus hesitated, then looked toward the stairway. "First, bring the children to Me." With that, He returned to the mat, sat down, crossed his legs, and leaned against the wall.

Abiah returned with the children, the boys walking behind her and Naomi holding her hand.

"Sit beside Me," Jesus said as He held His arms out to them.

Naomi released her mother's hand, ran across the room, and, very child-like, plopped herself down on His lap. The boys, reluctant to go to a stranger, hesitated until Abiah scooted them along.

"Come here, sit one on each side of Me. Please, do not be afraid," He said when they were seated.

He put His arms around their shoulders and pulled them close. Naomi leaned back against His chest.

"Children," He said, looking at each of them in turn, "hear My words and remember them in your heart. This day the Son of God is among you. Listen always to your parents, for they are wise and holy people. Love one another. No more pushing and fighting among yourselves. Be at peace, for the day has arrived, and your home is a place of sanctity. Serve your parents in their old age. Stand by them and all who are true to the faith of Almighty God. The blessings of the Lord are upon this home and all who live here. You are chosen at this young age to know the truth others have heard but not understood. I assure you of this; you will live in the kingdom of God through all eternity."

He looked at Mathan, then at Jacob.

"Tell me what it is that I have spoken to you."

The boys looked quizzically at each other, then Mathan responded, "Be good to each other and everybody else."

Young Jacob joined in, "And take care of our parents when they get old and be nice to everybody."

"You are wise children," Jesus said as He hugged each of them. "And you, my child?" He said to Naomi.

The young girl said nothing, but twisted around, put her arms around Jesus' neck, and hugged Him so tightly that He finally had to loosen her grip.

Jesus and his followers seated themselves around the table with the Master in the center against the wall. The women laid out the meal and went downstairs. Nur remained in the upper room to service the men when they ate the Passover meal.

After the meal, the women took the cups and dishes downstairs. Following the clearing of the table, Jesus summoned Nur to His side. "Go now and bring a loaf of unleavened bread. With it, bring a fresh cup of the best wine."

Nur went downstairs, and when he returned with the bread and wine, he saw Judas whispering to Jesus, who said something in return. Then Judas left the room.

With the bread and wine before Him, Jesus commanded the eleven remaining followers, "Now, be silent, and allow your heart and soul to partake of this divine moment." He held the bread and wine overhead, looked lovingly at each of them, and prayed, "Take this and divide it among you."

Placing the cup on the table and elevating the bread, He broke it and gave it to Peter, seated at His left.

With His voice uplifted, He said, "Take and eat. This is My body to be given up for you. Do this as a remembrance of Me."

Then He sipped from the cup and passed it to Peter.

When Peter drank from the cup, Jesus said, "This cup is the new covenant of My blood, which will be poured out for many for the forgiveness of sins. I tell you, I will not drink of the fruit of the vine again until I drink it with you in My Father's kingdom."

Nur witnessed each of these things silently—the coming of the Messiah and the fulfillment of the Scriptures.

After they consumed the bread and wine, Jesus once again called Nur, "Go now. Get a basin of water and bring it to Me."

Jesus rose from the place of honor at the table. Returning to the mat upon which He had been seated earlier, He scooted a bench in front of

Him. One at a time, the Master beckoned His followers to be seated on the bench. As they did so, he loosened the straps from their sandals and washed their feet, drying them with His garment. Upon completing the washing of their feet, He stood among them and spoke.

"Great trials and tribulations await you. Do not fear, for I am with you always." Looking from one to the other, He continued. "The greatest leader must be the most humble servant—the first shall be last, and the last shall be first." Continuing to make eye contact with each of them, He spoke in little more than a whisper. "Do not consider the vanity of vanities, for the Lord God knows your needs and hears your prayers. Be strong and accept the hand of God." Then the carpenter from Nazareth left the room, followed by the eleven.

Nicolas stood at the foot of the stairs. "Master, where are you going? The hour is late."

"We go to the Mount of Olives to pray," Jesus responded.

"Wait here for a moment, please," Nicolas said. He turned to a chest from which he pulled a magnificent robe of deep burgundy trimmed with a narrow band of gold and white threads. He placed it over Jesus' shoulders and snapped it with a golden clasp. "It is chilly, and You have no wrap. Here, take this. It is my finest garment, and I want You to have it."

"You're a good man, Nicolas. I'll forever remember your kindness."

Jesus encountered His mother standing near the gate with Nur at her side. He put His hands on her shoulders, paused, and looked into her eyes but said nothing. Then the Messiah left for the Mount of Olives.

The hours passed. Mary prayed until her eyes drooped, then fell asleep in the upper room. Nur sat in the courtyard, dozing, then praying for strength because he understood the Messiah's fate. Time slipped away, and suddenly he heard someone outside the gate.

"Hello, who is in there?" a young voice beckoned.

Nur jumped to his feet and went to the gate. Opening it, he found a boy no more than nine or ten years old, barefooted, and wearing an old, tattered tunic. His face was etched with fear—his hair wet with sweat, eyes wide in terror.

His voice quivered when he spoke. "They arrested your friend. A man named Peter told me to come for you."

"Tell me where," Nur barked.

"Sir, we were camped outside the walls when they brought Him by us. Only later, I found a man named Peter hiding under a tree. He was crying. 'I have denied Him,' he said. Then he told me to come here and find you or the man's mother." The child paused momentarily, caught his breath, and continued. "Is there anything else I am supposed to do?"

Nur thanked the boy for the message, then ran into the house, where he roused Nicolas and Ruth. He repeated the boy's words, then asked Ruth to wake Mary.

The early morning sun rose on the horizon when Mary, Nur, and the others arrived at Fortress Antonia. Soldiers at the gate told them Jesus was no longer there; He was under the authority of Herod Antipas at the Hasmonean Palace. They hurriedly went to the palace but found their way barred at the gates.

Crowds gathered nearby, but only a select few were allowed to enter the outer palace walls. Those few were soldiers or friends loyal to Herod. Within moments, a squad of soldiers exited the fortress with the beaten Messiah in their midst. His left eye had swollen shut. His lip was puffy and bruised from the beating the soldiers had administered. The hands and feet of the Messiah bore the wounds where the soldiers had used whips and barbs to defile Him.

Mary's heart was pierced as if by an arrow when she saw her Son. She gasped for breath; her knees buckled. Nur grabbed her around the waist and supported her as the horror she witnessed overwhelmed her.

When the soldiers escorted Him back to Pilate at Antonia, they continued to berate Him with taunts, spit on Him, and cursed His mother, who followed behind with Nur at her side.

Jesus staggered and stumbled along with His hands tied behind His back. The group moved slowly back to Antonia. Once again, Mary and

Nur could not enter the gate. They spent the remaining hours outside in prayer with their friends and other followers of Jesus.

Nur and Mary heard the masses inside the fortress calling for his crucifixion. Each time they heard the cry, "Crucify him," His family's hearts filled with grief and grace, for they understood the words of Scripture.

The noon hour approached when the fortress gates opened, and a squad of soldiers marched out, surrounding three men bearing crosses. The beaten and battered Messiah, upon whose head had been placed a crown of thorns, led the other two men to face execution. He shuffled His bare feet, having lost His sandals during the night.

Nur reacted quickly when Mary's knees buckled, grabbing her around the waist to prevent her from falling. They followed as closely to the condemned men as the soldiers would allow.

Bearing the weight of the cross and the sins for which He was sacrificing His life, Jesus faltered, stumbled, and fell against the cobblestone street. With each step, Mary and the others prayed aloud, seeking strength for Him and forgiveness for those who sinned against Him.

The condemned trio finally reached Golgotha, a small hill outside the city's gate. The condemned men and their followers stopped momentarily at the foot of the base of Golgotha. Nur looked at that otherwise nondescript little hill and recalled Jesus as a baby. He had cried out in His mother's arms when they passed by the place that would later become the site of His earthly death.

Jesus reached the hilltop first, with the other two men close behind. The soldiers lined the trail to the top, and only when the condemned reached the apex did the guards allow the family and a few close friends to approach the site of the crucifixion.

Nur's heart felt empty, but he supported Mary those last few steps to the hilltop.

The captain of the guard, a tall, solid centurion, reached around Jesus' neck and removed the robe from His shoulders. As this happened, Mary, Nur, and the others stood a few paces away, helpless to interfere with the fulfillment of Scripture. With little fanfare, two guards held Jesus by the arms as other soldiers placed the other condemned men on their crosses and hoisted them up to die slowly and painfully.

With that task complete, the captain turned and faced Jesus and His followers, bellowing, "Hail, King of the Jews." He laughed and spat at Jesus' feet, then mocked His mother. "Greetings to you, wretched woman." He gestured to her Son and again spat on Him. "If you had raised your child as a mother should, this would not be happening. Because of your failure, this bastard son of yours will die a cruel and miserable death."

The captain turned and nodded approval for the guards to fulfill their duty. Two of them stepped forward, lifted the cross from His shoulders, and threw it on the ground. Those holding Him by the arms kicked His legs from beneath Him, forcing Him to lie atop the cross. They lashed His arms to the crossbeam, then opened the palm of His right hand as another soldier stepped forward. The soldier removed a mallet and several large spikes from a bag around his waist. He paused for a moment and looked down at Jesus.

For the briefest moment, Nur thought the soldier had doubts about what he was about to do. Still, he hesitated no more than a heartbeat. Then, almost joyfully, he set about his task to deliver the nails into the body of the Son of God. Shirtless and with the muscles of an athlete, he leaned down, put a spike in the palm of Jesus' hand, and paused again. Then, with a sudden blow from his mallet, he drove the spike through Jesus' right hand and into the cross. Blood splayed across both men's bodies.

Jesus let forth a deep, guttural sound, gasped for breath, then suffered similarly as the man drove another spike into His left hand.

With Jesus' hands nailed securely into the cross, the guard stood upright and wiped his hands, then pointed to Jesus' feet, which the other guards bound together with a piece of rope.

Nur felt Mary's legs begin to sag again as the guard reached into his bag for the third spike, but she gathered her strength and watched the final nail pierce her Son's feet.

Nur cried as Jesus let out another deep wail and gasped as the guards stepped back to admire their work—the execution of Jesus of Nazareth, the Messiah, the Son of God.

The second team of soldiers and a small group of Roman slaves stepped around the crucified Christ and tipped the foot of the cross into a hole chiseled into the rocks, then hoisted it upright with an agonizing thud.

Jesus bellowed in pain as the foot of the cross fell in place. Blood dripped from His brow, into His eyes, and into His beard. The wounds on His hands and feet bled profusely down His beaten body onto the timbers and soaked into the soil below.

Nur observed in prayerful silence as several soldiers gathered in a circle and laughed, then scribbled on a scrap of wood, "King of the Jews." They ordered one of the slaves to climb a ladder and nail the inscription above Jesus' head. All the while, Jesus remained quiet, slowly looking about at those gathered there, some for enjoyment, some out of a sense of duty, some slaves, and some who believed in the one true God.

With the cross in place, several soldiers and townspeople examined the robe he wore. Without considering returning it to the family, an argument ensued about who could have it. The captain of the guard finally settled the dispute by retrieving a pair of dice from the saddlebag of his horse.

Nur and the others watched silently as this final humiliation occurred at the foot of the cross. The men took turns throwing the dice, laughing, and enjoying the sport about who would win the robe.

At mid-afternoon, the small entourage of faithful followers stood near the crucified Christ. Nur noticed that Mary had become stronger and more elegant than he had ever seen her. She stood tall and erect. A radiance glowed about her. She was a woman at peace with herself and with God in heaven. Others also noticed the change that came over her, even the captain of the guard, for Nur saw him whisper to his men, and they, in turn, looked at her and murmured among themselves.

As the day drew on, one of those crucified with Jesus turned to Him. With his lips dry and cracked, the thief uttered in a crackling voice, "Lord Jesus Christ, Son of God, Savior of the world, hear my prayer. Remember me when You enter paradise."

Mary, Nur, and all the others, including the soldiers, stood transfixed as Jesus turned His head to the thief. "This day, you will be with Me in paradise."

Goosebumps ran down the length of Nur's arms and legs. He saw the captain rub his eyes, discreetly drying a solitary tear that had formed there. Shortly thereafter, a storm cloud rose in the east and yet another in the west. Each moved slowly toward Jerusalem, roaring and tumbling black clouds, spewing lightning bolts to the ground. The wind began to howl. The clouds tumbled into one over the city. Flashes of rage erupted across the sky, and a deafening roar of thunder shook the hillside.

Jesus looked at His mother, who stood with John, Nur, and His followers. He spoke softly but clearly. "Mother, behold your sons! Sons, behold your mother!"

A torrent of rain, driven by a ferocious wind, raged upon them. Indescribable bolts of lightning flashed throughout the land.

Only the soldiers, Jesus' family, and His friends remained while the others fled. As the rain cleansed His body of the grime and filth of His tormentors, He raised His head into the wind and rain and cried out, *"Eli, Eli, lema sabachthani?"* (My God, My God. Why have You forsaken Me?)

Moments later, and for only the briefest instant, Nur and Jesus caught each other's eye, and they attained their life goals.

Then Jesus exhaled, lowered his head, and died.

Chapter Twenty
The Sepulcher

A wealthy man and a member of the Sanhedrin, Joseph of Arimathea, and his close friend, Nicodemus, stood stoically at the foot of Golgotha. As believers, the two men disapproved of those who voiced their intent to crucify Jesus. Nevertheless, they were powerless to stop the heinous act.

Aware of the approaching sunset signaling the start of the Sabbath and mindful of the adherence to Jewish law, Joseph knew burial of the dead must occur before the stars appeared in the night sky.

"There is no time to waste," he uttered softly.

Looking up into the sky, he saw storm clouds tumbling over the city from every direction. Hurrying to the palace, Joseph sought an audience with Pontius Pilate. With Pilate's permission, he would provide Jesus with the crypt which had been prepared as his personal tomb. It would be a high honor for the Messiah to find eternal rest in Joseph's own tomb.

If only, he thought.

Minutes later, he stood before the governor of Judea, Pontius Pilate. "Excellency," he said in his firm, masculine voice. "The man, Jesus—though a convicted criminal, he is a Jew." Adding a slight nod of deference to the governor, he smiled and continued. "It is necessary for the burial to take place before sunset. With your honorable permission, as a member of the Sanhedrin, I will take the necessary steps to assure his family their son will receive an appropriate burial."

Pilate chuckled. "You Jews and your laws. I have no desire to see where that criminal is buried. As far as I care, you can throw his body to the dogs." He coughed, spat into an urn beside his seat, then sipped a cup of wine from the table alongside his chair. "Be away with him. Do as you please."

Returning to Golgotha, Joseph saw Nicodemus and Jesus' friends and followers placing the cross on the ground and preparing to remove the spikes from His hands and feet. His mother, Mary, sat beside Him in the mud and coagulated blood that soaked the ground.

As their routine practice, the slave boys loaned their tools and experienced hands to the survivors of the crucified men. Without uttering a word, the first boy gave his claw hammer to John and, with a simple gesture, showed him how to pull the spikes from Jesus' hands and feet.

John held it firmly in his right hand, paused, and looked at the bloodied handle and hammerhead. Horror tore through his body as tears poured from his eyes. Gasping for breath, he glanced at the slave, who once again gestured the proper technique to pull the spikes free.

Then, as though in a rage, John went about his work. A mist of blood and water squirted over him, but he did not hesitate—he started and finished with one deep breath. With the last spike removed, John and Nur lifted His body and laid Him in His mother's arms.

Exhausted and emotionally drained, Mary wept softly and, with Nur's assistance, removed the crown of thorns from His bloodied and matted hair. Nur laid it aside as Mary leaned down and kissed her Son's forehead.

The Roman slaves stood silently and observed the family caring for the dead body. The second slave, a boy of about fifteen years, dabbed his eyes with the cuff of his garment. He spoke softly to his friends, "La pietà." His friends agreed with nearly imperceptible nods so as not to draw the soldiers' attention.

Joseph had remained silent, then bent over Mary's shoulder and whispered, "I am a friend. Please. May I escort your Son's body to a sepulcher? It is not far." Looking up at the darkening sky, he spoke again. "We must hurry before the Sabbath. A friend and I have fresh linen and oils by which we will cleanse Him before placing Him in my burial chamber."

Mary recognized Joseph—the father of the bride at the wedding in Cana. Forcing a hint of a smile, she nodded with tears streaming down her cheeks.

"You are an honorable man. Thank you. Your reward in heaven awaits you."

Martha, her sister Mary, and other women carefully wrapped His body in the fresh linens, then moved aside as Nur, John, Thomas, and James lifted the Messiah and carried Him on their shoulders to the sepulcher.

There was insufficient time to pray and anoint His body properly before placing Him in the tomb. Nevertheless, they performed a modicum of prayers before laying the Messiah in the sepulcher. Upon exiting the burial place, the four men looked at each other, then at the stone beside the entryway. Nur nodded and stepped forward with his shoulder against the rock. The others quickly joined him. With considerable effort and panting, they gradually rolled the heavy granite across the entryway.

A squad of soldiers took up guard near the tomb as a precaution against Jesus' followers who might steal His body in a scheme against the Romans or the Sanhedrin.

Despite their presence, sneers, and vile taunts, Mary gathered her friends around her and led them in a brief prayer after closing the sepulcher. "Our Holy Lord, we commit our lives and that of Your Beloved Son to You. We will not be discouraged by those who seek the vanity of vanities but will remain faithful to Your Holy Will."

With darkness sweeping across the land, Mary took Nur's hand like a mother to a child and led the entourage back to the home of Nicolas and Abiah.

Nicolas greeted them at the gate and led the men to the upper room. Abiah escorted Mary to a private room downstairs, where she assisted with cleansing the mother of the Son of God of the blood and grime of Golgotha.

After washing and dressing in clean, warm clothes, Mary ate some bread and sipped a cup of water. Exhausted, she and Abiah wrapped their arms around each other, huddled on a mat in the corner, and fell asleep.

Nur and the apostles, distraught, tired, and filthy, spoke little when they retired to the upper room. Accepting some bread and cheese from Nicolas and Mathan, each found a private spot in the room, collapsed onto the floor, and slept.

At the sound of the cock, Nur roused from the floor and looked around at his exhausted companions. Glancing about, he understood the thoughts and doubts that swept through their minds—*a flock without a shepherd.*

Tiptoeing among the sleeping men, he went to John in the far corner.

John opened his sleepy eyes when Nur nudged him. The apostle hesitated, focused his eyes, then whispered, "Nur, what do you want? It is too early to be up and about." He gestured to the others. "They need their sleep. Leave us alone."

"No," Nur whispered. "They can sleep, but not you or me. There is work to be done."

John bit his lip, propped himself against the wall, and stood straight, then nodded toward the door. "Outside."

The two tiptoed carefully over their sleeping friends, then went downstairs to the open courtyard.

Taking a cup of water from the shelf adjacent to the door, John guzzled it, replaced the cup, then looked at Nur. "What?" he barked.

"I can only tell you what I must," Nur replied. "I shall go to the synagogue to pray. His work is not yet done." He paused, breathed deeply, and put his hands on John's shoulders. "I know what I must do. I leave now but shall return in due time. Until then, John, be steadfast. Do not allow the others to weaken in this time of tribulation. But I must bow my head in the synagogue and pray."

"Have you lost your mind?" John snapped. "They hate us. They murdered the Son of God, and you want to pray in their midst?"

Nur stiffened his back and glared at John. "I know what I must do. You and the others stay here and rest, because trying times are at hand."

"Nur," John roared, "I have never understood you, and I certainly don't now." He shook his head dismissively. "Be about what you must." He breathed deeply and continued. "Jesus knew you better than the rest of us, so I must trust what you say." He gave the slightest hint of a smile. "When will you return? No one is safe here."

"I will take our mother to Ephesus. That was my command, and I shall see it through."

Chapter Twenty-One
Psalm Sixteen

Nur returned to Nicolas and Abiah's home on the midmorning of the third day after the crucifixion. Entering the courtyard, he found the children and a friend at play, running about and laughing—doing childish things, oblivious of the truth that swirled about them and all of creation.

He climbed the outside stairs to the upper room and found the apostles, Mary and her sister Martha, and Mary, the mother of the Messiah. Opening the door, the glory of God shone upon him as it did all of those present. Despite the horrors of Golgotha, their faces manifested His divine love. Their clothes shone as bright as the midday sun, and their voices resonated in praise and glory, for they had witnessed the fulfillment of Scripture.

Jesus' mother, wearing a white ankle-length gown with a powder blue veil over her hair and shoulders, greeted Nur with a smile and kissed his cheek, brushed his hair back, and held him in her arms. "He has risen," she exclaimed. "The words of the prophets have been fulfilled. Jesus, your brother and my Son, the only begotten Son of God, rose from the dead."

Nur stood motionless, looking at his mother with red, tear-filled eyes. His voice quaked when he spoke. "Mother, it is in Scripture—Psalm Sixteen, 'Nor will You allow Your Holy One to be corrupted.'"

Nur gave the slightest hint of a smile, nodded, and continued, "So it was written, and so it came to pass. He has risen to His Father in Heaven."

Mary wept as he held her close. Moments passed slowly, then she kissed his cheek again, led him into the main room, and called to the others, "Behold, our family is complete. Nur has returned."

She stood in majestic stature and gazed slowly, making eye contact with each of Jesus' followers. With her voice soft yet wielding the power of the Holy Spirit, she spoke. "From henceforth, each of you are my child. Jesus, the Word Incarnate, and I, His unworthy mother, declare that from this moment on, you and those who accept your teaching are my spiritual family—the children of God Almighty."

Having been perhaps the closest of the apostles to Jesus, John stepped forward and took Nur into his arms. "As I said before, Nur, I will never quite understand you." Stepping back at arm's length with his hands on Nur's shoulders, he looked intently at Jesus' brother. "I will never second-guess you, but you were not here when Jesus rose from the dead. Mary and Martha went to the sepulcher, but He had risen. Angels were there and spoke to them. 'He has risen,' they said. 'He is not here.' Oh, Nur. You, of all people, should have been there. You are His brother. He rose from the dead. The Messiah and our dear friend fulfilled the prophets' words, but you missed it."

Nur gracefully accepted John's rebuke, nodded, then spoke softly. "I had been at prayer in the synagogue. I understand no one approved of my absence, but I did what my heart and soul directed me to do."

Nicolas and Abiah brought water, bread, and some pomegranates to Mary and the others, then excused themselves.

All the apostles except John sat on the benches. Nur pulled up a mat where he and John sat on the floor. Mary removed some pillows from a shelf and arranged them so she could be seated next to John. Adhering to her Son's last command, she held John's hand and spoke. "Now, my son, tell us what we must do."

"The voice of the Father reaches out to all peoples," he replied. Taking a deep breath and pausing briefly to arrange his thoughts, he spoke with a gentle but commanding tone. "To all lands, here and across the Great Sea. We have much to do, for the Lord has appointed us as His messengers. The

Word of God must carry throughout the world. That is our commandment."

He glanced at Nur. "Your mission is to care for her," he said, gestur-
ing toward Mary. "It is not safe here. The Sanhedrin, the Pharisees, the
Scribes—Jesus challenged them, and they crucified Him. No harm shall
befall His blessed mother. The time is at hand. Leave!" His voice was
commanding as he continued. "Take her to Ephesus where she will be
safe."

Looking at his brethren, he continued. "We will take His Word throughout the lands, but Ephesus will be a place of warmth and refreshment." His
eyes fell upon the mother of the Messiah. "She is mother to each of us. At
her home, we will accept her love and guidance. Then, we shall again go
forward in fulfillment of the Scriptures."

Chapter Twenty-Two
Meryemana Evi

Nur made haste in preparation to close the house in Nain and make ready for the land and sea journey to Ephesus. Over the period of three Sabbaths, he arranged the sale of the home and property consisting of one hectare, six sheep, four hens, and one lovable old dog named Ontos.

Mary pleaded with Nur, "Please, son. Ontos is part of the family. He is strong enough to travel with us."

Taking her hands in his and smiling, Nur shook his head. "Mother, his hips trouble him. He would not survive the trip. Besides, Ontos watches over the sheep every night. He is good at it. He barks and chases off any would-be thieves or predators." Releasing her hands, he shrugged. "Ontos stays here. He has been a good dog and wonderful companion, but Ephesus is out of the question."

Mary bit her lip and nodded. "I know you are right, but I care for that old dog. I hate to leave him behind."

"Amos and Naama are familiar with him," Nur replied. "They bought the property and expressly asked if Ontos would stay with them. They, too, think he is a good dog. They will take care of him. He will remain their watchdog and be happy, so it all works out satisfactorily for all."

Mary looked down and, with pouted lips, said, "You're right. I know that. It is just so hard to leave this land and the people with whom we have lived for so many years."

With the help of Amos and his son, Abner, who provided two ox-driven carts to Caesarea, Mary, Nur, the sisters Martha and Mary, and their cousin Chava embarked on the long overland trek to the seaport.

There being no schedule of departures, Amos busied himself walking the quays and piers, inquiring about passage on a freighter. Late on the second day at the port, he encountered a ship's captain, Nyke, a tall, sinewy, dark-skinned Greek. He was readying his two-masted craft for the next voyage in which his only fare would be from passengers, plus an itemized list of charges for their cargo. Following a back-and-forth negotiation, they settled on a price that would encompass their entire trip, a long and slow three-week excursion to Cyprus, then to Miletus, and finally to Ephesus.

Chava had expressly asked to accompany them in the move to the foreign land. A fine seamstress, tent maker, and a believer in the Messiah, she had made many of Jesus' garments and would be a valuable benefit in serving the apostles' needs in the future.

They arrived in Ephesus on a beautiful, sunny day, three *shabuas* (weeks) after leaving Nain. Nur arranged lodging at an inn near the Agora Commercial District on the banks of the Cayster River which flowed into the Aegean Sea.

Yusuf, the innkeeper, one of Nur's acquaintances in the Ephesus region, had become a true believer in the Messiah, having heard stories from Nur and travelers from Judea. They told of His loving mercy, how He restored sight to the blind, cleansed lepers, and drove out demons. *Truly,* Yusuf knew in his heart and soul, *the Messiah has come.*

Following a good night's sleep in a real bed on dry land, the travelers rose with the morning sun shining brightly over their wonderful new homeland, Ephesus.

Yusuf had sent a late-night messenger to Athena and her family requesting they dispatch someone with a cart into the city to transport Mary to her new home.

The travelers had breakfast in Yusuf's fine dining room with fresh, hot *tijganites,* consisting of white flour and curdled milk, fried in olive oil and sweetened with honey. No sooner had they completed their meal than the clopping of horses' hoofs sounded in the courtyard—Alexandros and Philip were there.

Following a few minutes of greetings and good cheer, Nur and the two brothers moved the travelers' personal possessions into the carts, each pulled by a muscular, strong destrier: Alexandros' black stallion named Dynami (Power) and Philip's walnut brown stallion called Tachytita (Speed).

The household goods and luggage were loaded equally into the two-wheeled carts. Jesus' mother and Nur rode with Alexandros, while Martha, Mary, and Chava rode with Philip. The hour-long walk to Mary's new home was completed in a fraction of that time.

Leading the way, Alexandros brought Dynami to a halt when they reached the pathway up the hill from the road. Philip guided his cart to a standstill alongside his brother, allowing time for everyone to take in the magnificence of Athena and her sons' endeavors.

Mary alighted from the cart, kicked off her sandals, and rubbed her bare feet in the clean, well-groomed dirt of the lane. A beautiful smile swept across her face as tears of joy flowed down her cheeks. "My children," she said as she looked back from the house atop the hill to the men and women who accompanied her, "from God's kingdom in heaven to this sacred ground, we shall persevere in His work. The spirit of God Incarnate will go forth softly like the *ruah*—a breath of wind that cannot be seen but is true. It will travel the paths of the sea to touch all peoples throughout the world."

She inhaled the sweet smell of the spring wildflowers growing on the hillside. Glancing from one to another, then back to the colorful array that painted the countryside, she continued, "God's holy message will endure to the end of time."

Chapter Twenty-Three
New Apostles

At Athena's behest, Mary and her entourage spent their first three days resting, joining in communal prayer, and enjoying a purification bath.

In the early dawn of the second day, Mary wrapped herself in a towel and sat on a stone bench chiseled into the hillside. Her feet rested in a large, shallow clay dish. Using a pot of water she had heated over the fire, Athena slowly poured it over Mary's head and down her body, where the water collected in the dish.

Respecting her privacy, Athena stepped away while the mother of the Messiah used natron sourced from decaying wood and vegetable ash to cleanse her skin of the grime of her trip.

Mary, Martha and her sister Mary, Chava, and Athena each followed suit in purification bathing. From this time forward, they dedicated the Ephesus property to the service of the Almighty Father and His apostles who would fulfill their missionary efforts. Henceforth, this hillside compound became known as *Meryemana Evi* (Mother Mary's House).

The next day, Athena's four sons and Nur also carried out their purification bathing to complete the commitment to their Heavenly Father.

***

The household organized themselves by allocating time each day for their private and communal prayer and completing the chores of the estate—tend the sheep that had grown from a small flock to a substantial herd; prune and weed the garden and trees; purchase and weave the materials for Chava to make tents for the apostles to use during their visits at

Meryemana Evi; and go into the city on market days to buy or sell goods and attend the synagogue on the Sabbath.

*   *   *

The balmy spring months of *Iyar*, *Sivan*, and *Tammuz* eased into the warmer mid-year cycle of events of the *Tisha B'Av* Feast. During that period on a hot and blistering afternoon, the apostle John strode up the hillside path to Meryemana Evi. He had been at the foot of the cross with Nur when Jesus commanded them to provide care for His mother.

While pruning high in a fig tree, Nur caught a movement out of the corner of his eye. Balancing on a limb, he twisted around and saw John hunched forward with an old and battered leather pack on his back. With head bowed and his steps shuffled, he made his way toward the house, leaning on a walking stick for support. At the point of exhaustion, he manifested an unswerving commitment to fulfill the commands of his Savior.

"John," Nur shouted while he climbed down to the ground.

John looked up. Perspiration dripped from his brow, but a smile swept across his face. "Nur," he cried. "My beloved brother."

Nur dropped his shears to the ground as the two grasped each other at arm's length and wept openly. He removed the pack from John and, with the other arm wrapped around his brother's waist, led him to the shade of a eucalyptus tree where he kept a water jug in the shade. "Sit here," he said when John leaned back against the tree and allowed himself to slide gracefully to the ground. Nur handed the water jug to him, then turned toward the house and shouted, "Come. John is here."

Within moments, Athena flung the door open. Stepping out and seeing their visitor, she turned back into the house and called to the others.

Minutes later, all of them were gathered around John, laughing, crying, hugging, and lifting prayers of thanksgiving for the apostle's safe arrival.

Ever mindful of the importance of her support role, Chava removed the sandals from John's tired feet. Without hesitation, she dabbed her apron into the water jug and washed the apostle's feet. When she finished, she held his sandals up, inspected them, then tilted her head and smiled. "John, you have a broken strap. How did you walk in this?" she asked as she held it up to him for inspection.

John stretched his arms and legs, looked at his tired feet, and responded with a simple laugh. "Our Holy Father guides us and cares for us in the smallest ways we are never aware of." He glanced at his sandal in Chava's hand. "He brought me from Jerusalem with only one little broken strap. I'd say the Master takes good care of His servants."

"Brother," she replied, "yes, indeed. He does love us, but there is nothing wrong with being clean." At that, she snatched his pack and jumped up. "Your mother would never allow you to get your clothes so dirty. 'Shame on you,' she would say." She laughed and continued. "I am not your mother, but I'm taking your clothes and will launder them." Blowing him a kiss, she turned and ran up the hill to the mouth of the spring.

With Mary's motherly guidance, John blended into the daily activities of Meryemana Evi. He set aside daily time to pray and, periodically, to consult with Mary and Nur for the future evangelization plans for the apostles.

The months of *Elul* and *Tishrei* slipped away. More than most others, this day had been one of exceptional, strenuous labor. The heat sapped their strength as they picked figs and cleaned the irrigation ditch that fed the vineyard. After the sun peaked, they gave a light shear to the sheep to keep them comfortable for the remaining *Marcheshvan* period. However, in shearing, they had to be careful to leave enough wool to carry the animals through the cold of *Shevat* and into the following warm months.

Everyone was almost too tired from the day's chores to enjoy their evening meal. Though exhausted, they knew John had been deeply involved in prayer and study for the previous several days. Before their meal, he said he would have a statement for them after they had rested and refreshed themselves. Whatever pronouncement he might have, they knew it would be his decision about the next step in fulfilling Jesus' mission on earth.

Seated on a cushion at the head of the table, John cleared his throat and began. "My blessed family, we are God's gift to each other, but we must part company and surrender the remaining days of our lives to spreading His truth throughout the world."

He paused and looked first to Mary, then shifted his eyes slowly and methodically to Nur, Mary and Martha, Chava, Alexandros, Johannes, Philip, and finally to Didymus.

"My mother, and to all of you—my brothers and sisters—the time is at hand. The Lord God has brought us together to fulfill His wishes and to take His Word..." He hesitated, took a deep breath, and continued. "...to the ends of the earth. That was His command, and that is what we shall do. Each of us will use our God-given talents, sacrificing our lives, if need be, to spread His holy Word to everyone—Jews, gentiles, Greeks, Romans, slaves, pagans—to anyone and everyone.

"I'll stay here for a short time, praying and teaching God's Word in Ephesus. Then I must be on my way. I'll return as often as possible. My bones possess new vitality, for I am filled with the Holy Spirit." He glanced at each of them, smiled his ruddy smile, and continued. "I'm anxious to tell the world of the Lord God."

He paused and looked at Nur, then gestured toward the brothers, who were sitting expectantly.

"However, these men are not needed here any longer."

"Their mother?" Nur asked.

"She should stay and provide whatever help the mother of the Messiah requires, but her sons will find greater missions to accomplish—much more important than what they are now doing."

"What might that be?" Athena inquired.

John shrugged, tilted his head, and smiled at Athena. "Four strong, young men? Need I say more? They have not seen, yet they believe. With their faith and physical strength, they must go into the world and evangelize. They can do much more for our Father in heaven than tend to the animals and this house. Fishers of man shall be their new calling."

He looked at Nur, his expression gentle yet commanding. "As I say these words, I know deep in my heart that the Lord God sent this family to us from the first day you and Jesus found the ship tied up at the dock. From that precise moment, their mission on earth began. They shall take the Word of God into the world, giving their lives for it if need be."

Nur looked at John, then toward the brothers as they shuffled in their seats. He nodded in agreement. "Indeed, John, I know what you say is true. What good teachers they will be. We'll miss their company, but you are right. They must undertake a much greater mission—an undertaking for all mankind. Whoever receives the Word of God must share it with others. That is how it must be, for receiving the Word and holding it quietly in one's heart does not fulfill the call of the Holy Spirit. When a seed is planted, the person who plants it must nourish it, lest it die. They have received the seed. Let them go forward and nourish it."

"Until such time as they are well prepared," John replied, "you shall teach them of the one true God and His Son, Jesus, the Christ. You will know when they are ready. Until such time, you and they must spend your efforts to prepare them for the way ahead—a long and treacherous road."

The seasons of the year swept quickly through their lives. The brisk nights of fall gave way to the bone-numbing cold of winter. John, away much of the time, traveled throughout the land, teaching all who would listen to the Word of God. When he returned home, he spent equal parts of the day in prayer and in teaching the lessons of Jesus to the sons of Athena. When he and Nur were confident the brothers were ready for the hardships that lay ahead, he would send them into the world.

He spoke to them of the greed of Judas, the humility and honor of Mary Magdalene, and the miracle of the loaves and fishes on the shores of Tiberias. He told them of the second miracle of Cana in which Jesus cured the son of the high official, and the blessing of the Samaritan woman at Jacob's well. He told how Jesus raised Lazarus from the dead and of Jesus' travels throughout Galilee with people following Him from Decapolis and Jerusalem, Judea, and from beyond the Jordan, listening to His words.

John spoke of when Jesus saw the size of the multitude and climbed upon a mountain to speak these words that his disciples repeated many times:

> *"Blessed are the poor in spirit, for theirs is the kingdom of heaven. Blessed ared are they who mourn, for they shall be comforted.*
> *Blessed are they who hunger and thirst for righteousness, for they shall be filled.*
> *Blessed are the merciful, for they shall obtain mercy.*
> *Blessed are the pure in heart, for they shall see God.*
> *Blessed are the peacemakers, for they shall be called the children of God. Blessed are they who are persecuted for righteousness sake, for theirs is the kingdom of heaven. Blessed are ye when men shall revile you and persecute you and shall say all manner of evil against you falsely for My sake. Rejoice and be exceedingly glad, for great is your reward in heaven, for so persecuted the prophets which were before you."*

When John uttered these words, he foretold the lives and deaths that lay ahead for the brothers who accepted the Word, believing but not seeing.

Johannes and Philip were the first to leave, bound for Mytilene and Assos then to Troas, Neapolis, and Philippi. They would spend their lives traveling throughout Macedonia and Asia Minor, delivering the truth of the one Holy God. The night before their departure, as they prepared for their mission, the men joined Mary and the women, praying and singing songs of joy.

John gave them these final words of encouragement before snuffing out the last candle. "When Jesus entered the temple, they gave Him the book of the prophet Isaiah, and from it, He read:

"'The spirit of the Lord is upon Me; therefore, he has anointed Me. He has sent Me to bring glad tidings to the poor, to proclaim liberty to captives, recovery of sight to the blind, and release to prisoners.'"

John continued, "And to you, my brothers, so too do I say. The spirit of the Lord is upon you. Go in peace, for His angels shall watch over you forevermore."

John left Mary in the care of Nur, Athena, her two remaining sons, and Martha, Mary, and Chava. "You will know when the youngest is ready," he told Nur. "But don't let them leave a day before then. Teach him well, for he is eager. His brother will look after him, but I caution you. He is so young, like a young bull. He is ready to charge but not always sure why. Be observant but careful. He is too anxious. Caution him. Teach him. The world will not find salvation in a day or a year. He must slow down.

"When you are sure he is ready, allow them to go. And when they take their leave, send them to Judea. They will find the others, Luke and Matthew, who can use their help. The brothers are strong in spirit and back, and their enthusiasm will be good for Luke, who can be so somber. They will be good for him."

With that entreaty, John departed, leaving Nur the care and responsibility of the Blessed Virgin and the preparation of Didymus and Alexandros for their mission of salvation.

The weeks and months passed, and Didymus grew in age, wisdom, understanding, and patience. His brother, Alexandros, also developed in his role as a contemplative and loving brother. He would lead them into the most incredible journey of their lives—a journey far more significant than any voyage their father ever undertook.

When the time arrived, Nur gathered them for a final meal. Mary, the mother of Christ's church on earth, sat at the head of the table. Athena, the mother of God's newest emissaries, sat opposite her at the other end of the table. Her sons sat one at each side, midway between the two women whom they loved so much. The other women also sat at the table.

Nur, who always faded into the background and shadows, prepared and served the meal. Following the meal, he cleared the table, then set in its center a single candle. The last dim rays of the sun were on the distant horizon, and the luminescence of the candle cast a soft yellow glow on their faces. "Unto you, Alexandros and Didymus, I say these words my brother Jesus, the Anointed One, spoke. 'I am the Light of the World. No follower of Mine shall ever walk in darkness. No, he shall possess the Light of the World.'

"Another time he said, 'If you live according to My teaching, you are truly My disciples, then you shall know the truth, and the truth will set you free.'"

Nur moistened his lips and continued. "As Jesus is my brother, so too are you my brothers, for all mankind is brother and sister to each other. The leper, the blind, the naked, the poor, and the hungry. Those who are lonely and cry out for a gentle touch, a smile, or a word of friendship. Jews and gentiles, one and all."

Nur took two white candles, held their wicks to the flame of the burning candle, then gave one to each of his brothers. The candles' glow bathed the room in the brilliance of the wisdom and power of God.

Nur paused momentarily, then spoke. "Take the flame of the Lord and give light to the world, for the Holy Spirit is upon you. My brothers, I say unto you, the truth of the Most High has come to you. Go! Give to God all that you have, for your reward in heaven is great."

Alexandros rose, went to his mother, and kissed her cheek. He gave his candle to her and whispered into her ear, "Remember me in your prayers. I leave you in the flesh, but never in spirit."

He walked to the opposite end of the table and prostrated himself at the feet of the Virgin, who leaned forward and touched his soft hair.

"Pray for us, mother of the Son of God. We leave you now, but we shall never leave you, for you abide in our hearts."

"My son," Mary whispered, "you shall cast a long shadow over those who heed not our Lord and God, but your work will bring many to Him. Go now in peace, to love and serve the Lord."

As Alexandros arose, his younger brother got up and gave his candle to Mary, then prostrated himself at her feet. He spoke tremulously. "Blessed Mother, receive my candle. I go now to carry on the work of your child, my brother, Jesus Christ."

Mary leaned forward, her tears raining down on him. "My child, my sweet child. Your father and mother brought you into this world, and in his death, they brought you to my Son. Your heart is pure. Go now in peace to love and serve the Lord."

As the youngest of her sons came to her, Athena stood and embraced him. Tears trickled down her cheeks. "My son, my baby, my heart is filled with gladness, yet tears fill my eyes. Every minute of my life shall be of prayers for you and your brothers. Listen to Alexandros. Obey him. Learn from those who walked with Jesus. Go now, for the world is dark, but your words and deeds shall fill it with light."

Nur stood silently in the shadows of the room, listening and holding in his heart the truth of the one Most High.

Chapter Twenty-Four
Decalogue

Mary lived a life of joy and prayer. Each day became one of thanksgiving for her life as the mother of the Son of God.

Athena, Nur, and the others recognized their support role and tended the house and grounds so as not to interfere with Mary's prayers and contemplation. They joined her in morning and evening prayers. Still, she alone would go into the oratory, the room specially built for her private prayer and meditation.

Throughout the years, they hosted Jesus' followers with the simple joys of a home—a warm bed, good meals, and friends and family to share their burdens and their happiness. Luke arrived first, bringing them news of Alexandros' and Didymus' successes and how they had developed into a powerful team, delivering the Word of God.

Alexandros became a splendid preacher, and also manifested a long-range planning ability, deciding when and where they should go, and with whom and how they should approach different people. Didymus had become an excellent orator. His guidance captivated numerous men and women, Jews and gentiles alike, and held them spellbound to his words. He filled the hearts of many, and they received their baptism with water into what Didymus called "one holy catholic church, a church for all peoples throughout the world."

Athena's heart pounded with pride as she listened to him speak of how Didymus related the story of Moses and the Ten Commandments and how God Himself had cast them in stone, not just symbolically, for being cast in stone meant they were not negotiable nor to be compromised.

Alexandros, too, pierced the armor of the most hardened men with his explanations of the Decalogue, the "ten words" received by Moses on the mount. "Ten," he would say, "only ten words from the hand of God. Those and those alone are your obligations, your rights, and your way to salvation. And that is why the Holy Father sent His only begotten Son. As a people, we were deluged with laws developed by leaders from whom men and women sought guidance. Not that laws are bad, but when the abundance of laws and interpretations veil and obscure the truth, they must be done away with. Brothers and sisters, hear me! He came not to destroy, but to give life. His church on earth is not destroyed but has new life. It is born of flesh and blood of heaven's one and only God.

"Laws and rules give order for people. What has happened since the time of Moses is that good and honorable men have gone to the priest with their problems, saying what they thought they needed to do, but the solutions were against the laws of God and Moses. So the priests and elders explained how they could do what they wanted and still follow the laws. And these things became the rules, and years later other good men would come forward and need an explanation or exception to the rule, so another rule came along. The new rules lived from generation to generation, and now we have thousands of rules. But when we look to God, we find only ten. Men and women have come to a place in their lives where they are serving rules. They know the rules like they know their own children, but they do not know the Decalogue. It has been lost, buried by the authority of thousands of men over hundreds of years.

"So, God delivered His Son to guide us, to show us how to live. God is not against our leaders, but He will ravage those whose rules obscure His basic law—the ten words from the mount. Brothers and sisters, one and all, hear my words. When asked which of the commandments is the greatest, he replied, 'You shall love the Lord your God with all your heart, and with all your soul, and with all your might. This is the greatest and first commandment. And a second is like it: You shall love your neighbor as yourself. On these two commandments hang all the law and the prophets.'

"The Decalogue then is built on the twofold obligation of love of God and of all other people. If you fail to love anyone, you cannot love God. And it carries forward one more step. You must love God to enter the kingdom of heaven."

Following his discourse, Luke sat on a pillow and rested against the wall. He sipped a cup of wine Athena gave him, smiled, and looked into her eyes. "You and your sons will one day inherit the kingdom of God, for their feet will carry the word of God Almighty and His Son, Jesus, to the ends of the earth."

Chapter Twenty-Five
Words of the Master

The passage of time brought the apostles and many other disciples to Mary's door. Some were vigorous young men, others mature and stooped, but each was physically, mentally, and spiritually exhausted from the trials and tribulations of their work. It was at Meryemana Evi they received the blessings, guidance, and love that only a mother could give.

Matthew, the former tax collector under Herod Antipas, became a frequent visitor to Mary's house. He left his footprints behind as he traveled throughout Galatia and on to Macedonia, constantly on the move to find new souls to baptize and to mentor others who had become followers of Jesus the Christ.

Matthew, educated and physically strong, learned that many men who favored the caste systems found him to their liking and would listen intently to his words of salvation. He spoke the way they spoke and understood their reliance on material things. After hearing his words, however, they understood the true importance of life, the vanity of vanities, and how their drive for material things could separate them from the Lord God.

"Listen," he said, "to the very words spoken by the Master:

'Ye rich men, weep and howl for your miseries that shall come upon you.

Your riches are corrupted, and your garments are moth-eaten.

Your gold and silver is cankered, and the rust of them shall be a witness against you and shall eat your flesh as it were fire.

Ye have heaped treasure together for the last days.

Behold the hire of the laborers who have reaped down your fields, which is of you kept back by fraud, crieth: and the cries of them which have reaped are entered into the ears of the Lord of Sabaoth.

Ye have lived in pleasure on the earth and been wanton; ye have nourished your hearts as in a day of slaughter.

Ye have condemned and killed the just, and he doth not resist you.'

"And the Master told them:

'It is easier for a camel to pass through the eye of a needle than for a rich man to enter into the kingdom of heaven.'"

Men trembled when he said these things. It seemed as though Matthew and Jesus were speaking directly to each of them. Many converted to the true God through these words and came to enjoy Matthew's company and enlightened conversation.

Mary, too, enjoyed his company, a blend of joyful prayer and meditative conversation. It was mesmerizing for her to hear his understanding of the Scriptures and their meaning for Jews and gentiles alike. His education and work for Herod, followed by his meeting and acceptance of Jesus as the Son of God, gave him an uncanny ability to move freely among people, to understand them, and to open their hearts at the same time.

"If I can just plant the seed," he would say, "they will harvest the fruit of the vine."

Matthew's love of Mary and her Holy Son nourished his life from dawn to dusk, summer to winter, and desert to the mountaintop. He committed his life to fulfill the call of the Messiah.

Johannes and Philip, too, enjoyed many successes as they carried the Word throughout the land, baptizing in the name of the Father, the Son, and the Holy Spirit. They found strength in each other's company and nourishment in their understanding of the Scriptures. Johannes often led their preaching, delving into the Psalms, showing to one and all the truth of Almighty God. As his lessons took them to the scriptural peak, Philip joined in. With his guidance, the audience understood the truth of God, the Scriptures, and how they were fulfilled in the coming of Jesus—a man with no interest in armies or palaces nor interest in having lofty status or civil authority. A man, yet the Son of God, He came to be a servant for all people, a man who showed them how to live and die. Divine, yet human, He walked among them. He taught His followers to go into the far reaches of the world, to bring all men together under the mantle of His protection for a life of eternal peace. When people asked the brothers about *their* God and who could abide in His eternal kingdom, the brothers turned to the Psalms, saying:

"He that walketh uprightly, and worketh righteousness, and speaketh the truth in his heart.

He that backbiteth not with his tongue, nor doeth evil to his neighbor.

Nor taketh up a reproach against his neighbor.

In whose eyes a vile person is condemned, but he honoreth them that fear the Lord.

He that sweareth to his own hurt, and changeth not.

He that putteth not out his money to usury, nor taketh reward against the innocent. He that doeth these things shall never be moved."

When the people asked of them, "Is there not more?" the brothers responded again with the Psalm of David.

"Praise ye the Lord,

Sing unto the Lord a new song, and His praise in the congregation of saints.

Praise God in His sanctuary; praise Him in the firmament of His power.

Praise Him for His mighty acts; praise Him according to His excellent greatness.

Praise Him with the sound of the trumpet; praise Him with the psaltery and harp.

Praise Him with the timbrel and dance; praise Him with stringed instruments and organs.

Praise Him upon the loud cymbals; praise Him upon the high-sounding cymbals.

Let everything that hath breath praise the Lord.

Praise ye the Lord."

The summers passed into winters, and the years went by. Mary achieved her life's mission, not only by bearing the living Son of God, but also by nurturing His followers when they were tired and hungry or in need of her prayers and guidance. She followed closely the life of John, a young man who had been an apostle of Jesus, full of zeal, who preached the Word throughout Palestine and Asia Minor, who the Romans later banished to Patmos. Eventually, he made his way to Mary in Ephesus and from there wrote many of his works.

She later learned of the fate of Andrew, who suffered crucifixion at Patras on an X-shaped cross. She wept bitterly, not only for his suffering, but even more so for the tragic sin of those who committed that horrible deed.

"If they seek not the Lord's forgiveness," she said to Nur, "then surely they will suffer eternal damnation for their sins. So for them, too, I weep."

Many years later, she met Luke and Paul. The two apostles had met in Troas and spent much of their time preaching and writing as they traveled throughout Asia, Greece, and Macedonia. A learned man and a physician, Luke became a follower of Paul. Eventually, he took up the same mission of delivering the truth to Romans, Greeks, and people of all races. Luke accompanied Paul during his last imprisonment and brought the word of his death to Mary and Nur.

Peter converted Mark, a Hellenist, and Mark often sought rest and comfort in Ephesus. A frail but studious man, Mark's trips between Jerusalem and Antioch and throughout Asia Minor wore terribly on him. However, in the comfort of Mary's home, he regained his physical and spiritual strength, then would leave again to carry the power of the Holy Spirit to all who would listen.

Of them all, Simon Peter most amazed Mary. His name came from the Greek word *petros,* which means "rock." A man of uncompromising conviction, he never tired spiritually or physically, even when he appeared unable to walk another step. His far-ranging travels brought him to her door many times, but he seldom lingered more than a night.

"Blessed Mother," he would say, "your warmth and kindness, and Athena's fine meals, are temptation enough, but I cannot stay. My life on this earth is not infinite, and there is so much work to do. I must go."

Before he left the doorstep, he fell to his knees at her feet, and Nur watched in prayerful silence as Mary gave him the blessing of the Most High. She placed her hands upon his head and whispered a soft prayer. When she finished, she leaned down and kissed him.

"Go then, my child, my rock, my fortress, for the glory of God is upon thee. Deliver the Holy Spirit to all of my children."

Chapter Twenty-Six
Alpha and Omega

At sixty-four years of age, Mary's life attained fulfillment. She had given strength and courage to her Son's followers for sixteen years, feeding their tired and exhausted bodies, counseling and praying with them, and offering her motherly love. When she accomplished her destiny, she yielded her body and soul to God.

Athena and Nur, along with several women followers, were with her during her final days. While neither sick nor broken, the Holy Spirit filled her body and soul. Mary took to her bedroom while friends tended to her day and night, feeding her soup and bits of bread. Athena dabbed her forehead with a damp cloth to refresh her against the relentless heat of the sun, and the other women gathered about her in prayer, giving her what comfort they could, for she was Mary, the Queen of Peace, the mother of the Word Incarnate.

In the dignity of approaching death, she led them in prayer even though her voice had become weak and nearly inaudible. "My Lord and my God," she prayed, "give us this day our daily bread. Forgive us our trespasses as we forgive those who trespass against us. Lead us not into temptation but deliver us from evil. For thine is the kingdom, and the power, and the glory, now and forever, amen."

As the night grew on, Nur knelt silently in prayer at her bedside. She looked at him, smiled, and surrendered her will to God.

Athena and the other women wailed and cried out, "Blessed be the name of Jesus. Blessed be the name of Mary. Blessed be God."

They prayed at her bedside throughout the night, lighting luminaries and placing them at the head and foot of her bed. The lights threw a peaceful glow over the room, and the presence of the Holy Spirit filled everyone there.

As she had requested, they dressed her in a blue gown tied at the waist with a white silk cord. They placed a white mantle over her hair and draped it to the tips of her fingers. Slippers were placed on her feet, and as she lay on her bed, they covered her with a white altar cloth they had removed from her oratory.

After the morning sun crested the distant hills, the women and men from the area came to pay their respects and pray. When the afternoon shadows were long and the time for her burial arrived, the women looked about for Nur, but could not find him. They expected him to lead the men who would carry her body to the hillside crypt they had prepared to receive her.

"Alas," Athena cried out, "after Jesus' crucifixion, it was too great a burden for Nur to bear, so he went away to pray and grieve in private. And now," she said to the others as she wept, "once again we need him, but he's gone." She paused and dabbed her eyes with her cuff, then continued. "Come," she directed to the men, "I will lead you. Come now, for the time of her burial has arrived."

With pious dignity, they placed the body of the mother of the Messiah on the mahogany bench they'd brought from their home in Nain. Athena led the way, and the men carried her remains. The women walked alongside, carrying incense and singing the praises of God. When they reached the site of the tomb, they placed her on the stone slab carved into the side of the sepulcher. In humble decorum, they bowed down, then left her body there and placed boulders across the entrance of her tomb.

Mary, the daughter of Joachim and Anne, the wife of Joseph the carpenter, the mother of Jesus, the Messiah, had surrendered her earthly life.

The men, women, and children who accompanied her body to the grave remained there until nightfall, singing and celebrating her life with prayers of thanksgiving. The late afternoon breeze refreshed them as the sun cast its last glimmer of light over the horizon, then slipped into the darkness of the unknown. The day was gone, and the dark of night fell over Ephesus.

Shem, an older man of devout faith, broke the silence. "What is that?" he asked, pointing to the sky, his voice weak from hours of weeping and praying. The others looked into the sky and saw a star growing in size and brilliance and spinning as it plummeted toward the earth. The ground quaked. Clouds appeared in the sky, spewing bolts of lightning. Thunder pealed and echoed across the valley. A fierce wind swept across the land. Cattle and sheep began to bawl, roosters crowed, and the fear of the Lord overcame the people at the gravesite. The men and women threw themselves prostrate onto the ground, crying out to the Lord God to save them.

Suddenly, a peaceful silence fell over the land. The wind calmed, and the clouds parted, leaving a new star shining brightly above them. Its glow lit the hillside with a bluish hue, and the sweet scent of roses filled the air.

Lifting himself up from the ground, Shem looked toward the star. "Arise," he commanded. "Arise, for the power and glory of God is upon us this moment."

As he uttered those words, the star again began spinning vibrantly in the sky and became even more brilliant in color, then swept down upon them. Suddenly, it transformed before their eyes. It was Nur, an angel of the Lord. His glow swept over the hillside and valleys as he descended from heaven. An aura of love and peace swept over all living things. Again, the prayerful people fell to the ground in fear, but he spoke to them as he stood in the sky surrounded by the cherubim and seraphim.

"Arise, people of God. Do not be afraid, for the blessing of the Most High is upon you now and forever. Go in peace to love and serve the Lord." As he said these words, the angel Nur turned to the tomb and breathed upon it, blowing the boulders away and casting them down the hillside. He stepped to the entrance and shouted out, "Mary, mother of the Son of God, arise!"

The faithful followers of Jesus and Mary trembled in apprehension as a luminous glow radiated from the grave, and multitudes of angels filled the heavens, singing, "Glory to God in the highest. Blessed be the name of God. Blessed be Mary, the mother of Jesus." Their hymns fell to a soft chorus of praise as Mary appeared at the entrance, clothed in white garments brighter than the sun.

"Peace to you," she said when Athena and the others once again fell to their knees in fear. "Thank you for having heard our prayers and following my Blessed Son, for your reward shall be eternal life in the Kingdom of Heaven." Nur moved toward her, took her hand in his, and they ascended together to heaven. Angels greater in number than could be counted in a lifetime filled the heavens. They parted as Mary and Nur approached.

Before her, Mary saw her Son, Jesus, and at His side, her faithful husband, Joseph. Tears of joy flowed from her eyes.

Jesus stepped forward and placed his gentle hands on her cheeks. "Mother," he said, "I present to you My Father."

Jesus and Joseph stepped aside, and Mary looked upon the face of God.

The multitude of angels sang the praise of God, His Son, Jesus, and His mother, Mary.

The Lord God led her to His throne, accepting from the Archangel Michael a golden crown studded with jewels and beautiful stones and placing it upon her head. The Archangel Gabriel offered Him a Lily of the Valley, and God placed it into her folded hands. A young seraph placed a bouquet of red roses at her feet.

Then the Lord God spoke to her. "Mary, you have served Me well and shall be known forevermore as the Queen of Heaven. Whatever you ask of Me for the faithful on earth, that shall I do."

The angels and archangels, the cherubim and seraphim, the dominions and powers, the virtues and thrones, the principalities and saints in heaven rejoiced, for the glory of God was complete.

Ἄλφα και το Ωμέγα

About the Author

Thomas J. (Tom) Nichols lived in Tucson, Arizona, where he spent a vital part of his life at a Catholic Orphanage. Upon graduation from high school, he served in the USMC before joining the Tucson Police Department. He retired as Deputy Chief, then as Chief of Police in Lubbock, Texas, and later at the Lubbock Independent School District.

Tom's police career ranged from patrol, detective, Sergeant, Lieutenant, Captain, Deputy Chief, and Chief of Police. During those years, he researched and published numerous articles and papers on Community Oriented Police, police policies and procedures, and the role of police officers in public schools.

Tom graduated from the University of Arizona Bachelor of Science, Magna Cum Laude. He also graduated from the FBI National Academy, FBI Executive Development Program, the Senior Management Institute for Police at Harvard University, and numerous other programs and institutions. Upon retirement, he held a Master Peace Officer Certification from the Texas Commission on Law Enforcement.

Tom is committed to local, regional, and international church affairs. Traveling with his wife, Gwen, who serves as his editor, they lived the richness of the sights and sounds of Ireland and Scotland, the historic cathedrals of Eastern Europe, and the Orthodox churches of Russia. Even more fulfilling was the experience of the Holy Land—the Church of the Nativity, the Holy Sepulcher, The Annunciation, the Mount of Olives, the River Jordan, Capernaum, Tiberias, the Sea of Gallie, Jericho, and Ephesus. Last but not least was a trip to Ars, France, and the site of the *"Curé d'Ars,"* Jean Baptiste Marie Vinney.

The author has previously published seven novels and three short stories, of which two have supernatural themes. You can find out more on Tom's website: www.thomasjnichols.com/

Keep in Touch

Please visit me online:
Website: www.ThomasJNichols.com.

Blog
ThomasJNichols.blogspot.com

You can sign up for my newsletter on my website and receive a free short story called, Come Back Yesterday. I share monthly news, special offers, and early previews of my upcoming releases.

Social Media:

Facebook: ThomasJNicholsAuthor

Twitter: @Tomas0274

Instagram: eljefe274

Linkedin: thomas-nichols-682556b